MW01204573

Nicolette's Quarters

Written by

Vicky Ann Baur

DEDICATION

To my friends who encouraged me, who I won't name but know who they are. You were there with me during the day and night when I needed to bounce ideas around. You were also there to read my drafts and redrafts and offer valuable feedback.

Also, to my deceased stepmother Marlene, who was my biggest fan. When I was eleven, she handed me a thick hardcover book full of blank pages. The cover was full of Winnie-the-Pooh images. She handed it to me and said, "Here, you are a writer so go write." So, I did.

ISBN: 9798621111533
Imprint: Independently published

Chapter One

The knob felt cold in her hand. She gripped both of her tiny hands around it and pulled. It was so dark she could barely see the sidewalk down the center of the front yard. Stepping onto the concrete slab carefully one foot at a time, she glanced around the yard. Relying on the moonlight to guide her forward, she left the front door wide open on its hinges. The grit of the sidewalk was scratchy on the bottoms of her bare feet. As she neared the center of the yard, she looked up at the large oak tree that grew tall above her. As she brought her gaze back down towards the street a strange rusty-colored car pulled up to the curb directly in front of her path and stopped. As she neared the passenger side door the tension and fear built inside her and for a moment something told her to run back to the house. Before she could turn to run, the window lowered quickly and two shadowy male figures were revealed. The one nearest to her reached his arms out of the car window and threw a snarling cat directly at the child's face and she fell to the ground in horror.

Nicolette suddenly screamed out into her dark bedroom as she woke from her nightmare. As she glanced around, she noticed the bulb from the night light on her Winnie the Pooh lamp cast eerie shadows onto the walls and it heightened her terror she still felt by what she had just experienced. Realizing the men, the car, and the cat must have been another one of her common nightmares she sat up and called for her mother three times. Her quivering voice got a little louder each time it went unanswered. If she wanted her mother, she would have to get off her bed without the scary monsters reaching out and grabbing her ankle. Avoiding the open closet door where the goblins watched her from at night would be tricky. If she could just get to her closed bedroom door and get it open quickly enough, she could run to her parent's bedroom and her mother would hold her and make it all go away. Nicolette looked down to the floor on each side of her bed terrified of seeing a face pop out and scare her. Deciding it was too risky she laid back on her pillow and balled up under her blanket. She was careful to not let a hand or foot or even a strand of her long blonde hair hang off the side for the monsters to pull on and she cried herself back to sleep.

The next time Nicolette opened her eyes, the sun was blazing through her white curtains showing off the embroidered Winnie the pooh figures floating from red balloons on each side of the window. In the daylight, her room was bright and cheery with all of her favorite things around her. A bookshelf was bursting with fun books to read. A small wooden box resembling a small suitcase with a handle sat near a table. Inside the two flip-up latches was a vinyl turntable. She had several storybook records and could often be found sitting on the floor listening to them while she turned the pages of the attached book and followed along. There was a table full of coloring books, crayons, and watercolor paints. A glass of water sat near the edge holding some brushes. Nicolette loved to color, draw and paint. The evidence of this hung from her bedroom walls with tacks and tape. The closet wasn't scary in the daytime either, she swung it open and pulled down her favorite dress, struggled to get it on straight and slipped on her sandals. Although she still had a tinge of leeriness towards the under part of her bed, she made a wide enough circle around it to get to the door, open it and head out to the kitchen. Her stomach was grumbling.

Nicolette was tiny but fierce. Unfortunately, at her young age, she had to be. She liked to do everything herself. Make her cereal, get herself dressed and choose her own activities. If she had to ask for help it felt like an insult. If she didn't ask and someone tried to help her it was worse. Being the youngest of three children she fended for herself a lot. Since she was tough and capable, she was left to her own devices most of the time. She looked up to her big brother Gerald as her own personal hero. He always looked out for her. She was the closest to a little brother he was ever going to get. Although he was more than twice her age, he taught her to play football, all of the team names, and they would draw and color in the helmets together on rainy days stuck indoors. When the neighborhood kids gathered to ride bikes or make go-carts and race Nicolette was always Gerald's fearless driver. He could roll her down the biggest hill at the park in a rickety go-cart with no breaks and she cheered and reveled in it, taking home the first-place ribbon made from construction paper every time. Her sister was only a couple of years older and they didn't have much in common. Nicolette was the daredevil driver and Angie made the ribbons. They played barbies together sometimes, but Angie was more of a girly-girl who didn't like to get dirty and she constantly combed her hair especially her bangs ad nauseam. Thankfully they didn't share a room anymore. Angie's room had a boring frilly bedspread, pillow shams and dolls staged carefully in a rocking chair. It was too clean as if no one lived in it. Nicolette preferred her own room, with art, books, and music. Her room was messy, but she knew where everything was. It seemed as though the only thing Angie did was play dress up and tell stories. Boring stories that seemed to go on forever.

Nicolette's parents had a tumultuous relationship and the house usually appeared as if no adults actually lived there. It was tidy though and although her mother was constantly busy, she appeared from the basement, laundry room, her bedroom, or the outside garden to wrangle Nicolette down a few times a day and make her eat. Nicolette's appetite was very small. She was petite and although very thin, she was nothing but athletic muscle. Her Dad was at work long days and at the bar most nights during the week. When he got home it was better to tiptoe carefully around him because he was usually angry about something. Since she was a little wild and full of energy Nicolette had been on the receiving end of his wrath all too many times when one of her great ideas turned out to be a bad one. One time she decided it would be a good idea to climb the apple tree with a potato peeler and get the gross green skin of the apple and sit up there to eat it in peace. The only problem was, she sliced a flap of skin from her index finger with the first cut and wailed as the blood rushed down her hand and arm dripping on her clothes. Her Dad was the one who had to retrieve her from the tree limb as she sobbed and rather than comfort her, he yelled at her and called her stupid like he often did. If she could get out of it without him dragging her by her arm to her bedroom and spanking her until she was broken it was a win. He would only stop when she curled up in fetal position sobbing so hard, she visibly shivered and her breath skipped beats on its way in and out of her lungs.

The weekends were usually fun. Her mother's family lived a couple of hours away but had lots of family on her Dad's side nearby who liked to gather at their house, barbecue and tell stories about the past and what was new in their lives. Cousins and neighborhood kids would gather and play games in the yard, run through the sprinklers and eat popsicles until they were all rainbow-colored from lips to clothes. It was fun listening to her grandparents tell their stories and make everybody laugh. She loved it when the stories were about her. Like the time Nicolette jumped up to see inside a garage window, her parents were looking into and instead of getting to see anything inside, she got an eye full of the lit cigarette her mother was holding. An emergency room visit, some eye medicine and a full gauze eye patch for a week and she was good as new. Nicolette even let her mother help her cut her meat at dinner time that week.

The other story her mother loved to tell about her was the day she came into the world. It was a little awkward each time Nicolette had to hear how she wasn't supposed to be born. Her parents weren't shy about announcing they never wanted her. Once she got past the sting of that fact the rest of the story made Nicolette sound fierce and strong and she liked that part. Each time she heard the story repeated the sting lasted less and less as she got older. After all, with the fate of her parents' marriage in constant peril, they just didn't want any more children. Her mother was using an IUD at the time she got pregnant and they say Nicolette was so determined she pushed right through it. Her mother was horrified the whole pregnancy, crying and wishing it wasn't happening.

Her parents did a lot of fighting while Nicolette was in the womb. It is probably why on her birthday Nicolette came out screaming and pushing people away. She didn't want to be breastfed or be held closely and rocked by her mother. Her Dad nicknamed her cockroach because he figured Nicolette could survive the apocalypse out of sheer strength and stubbornness while others perished around her.

After Nicolette finished her cereal, she hurried out the back door to see her mother set up for one of those family barbecues and realized it must be the weekend. Everyone was due to show up around eleven or twelve so she had to stay in the yard instead of going to the park or a friend's house. Nicolette kept herself busy shoveling holes in the dirt, collecting leaves, playing with inchworms and smelling the flowers on the lilac bushes and in her mother's garden. Soon her grandparents, aunts and uncles, and cousins began arriving. Nicolette and her cousins couldn't wait until their uncle Felix showed up. He usually came a little later than everyone else. Possibly he enjoyed making a grand entrance. He was well dressed, classy, drove a ritzy car, and made the kids laugh a lot. By the things he said and the possessions he owned, they all knew he had a lot of money and he was generous with it on birthdays and at Christmas time. They would all run towards him fidgeting in their shoes waiting for him to get out of the car. While the boys inspected his wheels and paint job on his car, the girls ran to hug his leg or waist depending on their height. He would bend down and point to his cheek. Each girl would give him a peck on the cheek and he would give them a dime in return. They would run off giggling. He always asked Nicolette for two and she got a quarter.

"Shhhh," he'd say.

Every time he would tell her not to tell and raise his index finger to his pursed lips, she felt special. He told her if the others got jealous, he would have to start giving her only a dime. Nicolette learned then it pays to stay silent and so she did. She would pop the quarter in her pocket if she had one and run off to play.

After the adults were tired of sitting around the picnic table the men would break off and sit in lawn chairs in the yard, while the women kept themselves busy gabbing and cleaning up dishes, making desserts and assisting with the kids. Uncle Felix motioned to Nicolette to come to sit on his lap as he had pretty much ever since she was out of diapers. If they were at his home, she was the one he had to sit with him in his big plush king's throne type chair while everyone watched movies together or ate from tv trays around them. She felt like the queen in the room.

Nicolette happily galloped across the lawn, twirled her Winnie the Pooh dress in front of his chair as she turned around to back towards him so he could pick her up and slide her onto his lap. He put one hand on her arm and the other hand cupped between her legs to lift her with it. Sometimes it was a little uncomfortable when he held her that way because his hands were strong and large, but if his fingers hit her panties a certain way it made her feel a strange tingle between her legs and kind of liked it. Since she was small certain men picked her up that way. She had learned she had to wait for them to call her over to sit with them though. It confused her when she'd ask to get on their laps and they looked embarrassed and told her to go play. She would innocently beg them to pick her up and pull their hand towards her pelvis and sometimes they would get mad and shoo her away. It made her feel a weight of rejection she did not enjoy but had become accustomed to. People seemed to be compelled to comment on her beauty and her strength and what a great woman she would grow up to be. Yet they were quick to put her in her place and discard her when it wasn't convenient. It was a common theme to be woven throughout her life.

After Nicolette was planted on Uncle Felix's lap, he rested his hand on her thigh. As she had done before, she took his hand and pull it back for another tingle. Sometimes he would slip a finger under her panties to touch her skin down there directly and she would fidget. All of the other men were too busy out-talking each other, laughing, drinking beer, and smoking cigarettes to notice. If someone approached their chair his hand would quickly come out from under the flap of her dress and he would put her down and pat her on her bottom to go play. This time her cousin came running up calling Nicolette's name to hurry up because the group of kids was walking to the park to use the playground. She jumped off of Uncle Felix's lap and ran off to join them.

Chapter Two

Eventually, Nicolette became leery of certain men and by then she was too big to be picked up and sit on laps anyway, but she felt less special and occasionally she searched for ways to feel the strange tingle on her own. It wasn't the same when she touched herself as when they touched her. At a certain age, Uncle Felix stopped paying the girls for kisses. He would just pull out his empty pocket from his trousers and say he was broke. The kids knew he wasn't, but they figured he finally listened to the aunts one of the times they told him to stop doing that because it was teaching them the wrong things. Nicolette missed the coins but quickly adjusted to the change.

Now that Nicolette and her siblings were getting older their mother decided to take on a job as a waitress at a local steak house. Her mother would sleep later in the mornings and be pretty grouchy during the daytime. She spent a lot of time on the phone smoking cigarettes when she was home. If Nicolette wanted to get her mother's attention while she was on the phone, she would have to call her by her first name instead of Mom.

"Mom…Mom…Mom…VALERIE!!" she'd say.

Her Mom would angrily ask what she wanted although not pay attention to the answer and then shoo her away. Nicolette stopped trying to talk to her after enough times being rejected. Nicolette started referring to her mother as Valerie on a regular basis. She didn't think the term Mom fit her very much anymore.

Valerie had met a new friend at the steak house. His name was Mitchell. He had a certain happy glow about him Nicolette wasn't used to. He was very handsome and treated Nicolette very respectfully. She sort-of developed an eight-year-old type of crush on him and she could tell her mother had the thirty-five-year-old type of crush on him. He would come over to the house while their father was at work. His presence made the whole house feel different. To Nicolette, it seemed suddenly warmer, gentler, and kinder the moment he walked in. When Mitchell was around it was pretty much the only time Nicolette saw Valerie smile or laugh anymore.

Nicolette had always thought her mother was the most beautiful woman in the world. She described her that way to her friends at school. Valerie had lost weight and seemed to have a steady diet of Pepsi and cereal. The kids ate a lot of TV dinners and other things they could make themselves. Their Dad still went to the bar after work most nights so sometimes Mitchell would stay the whole afternoon and take Nicolette and the rest of the family for burgers and ice cream in his quirky orange Volkswagen van.

Nicolette loved the van. It was way cooler than a school bus and it had three big windows on either side and one on the back. She loved getting to open the large sliding door for everyone to get in. She would kneel between the two front seats and lean on the armrests to be the navigator. She leaned closer to Mitchell. Being around him made her feel safe. At times she fantasized what it would be like if he was her father. She imagined how much happier they would all be. Maybe then she would be able to call Valerie Mom again.

One-night Mitchell took them all for their usual burgers and ice cream. Mitchell drove and Nicolette navigated. It was raining pretty hard and the lightning forked down to the ground in the distance. Nicolette always tried to determine if it ever struck anything and if so what it hit and how big was the fire. The wipers scratched back and forth on the large front window of the van. When they arrived at the Dairy Queen. Mitchell came around and slid the side door wide open. Like a gentleman, he helped Nicolette and Angie down to the ground. Gerald was fourteen so he hopped out himself and slid the door slamming it closed. Mitchell patted Gerald's back as if to say he approved of him and kept it there while they all walked together and into the restaurant. They ordered and ate their burgers. Nicolette kept pestering Mitchell to play pinball with her and he obliged. She liked it when an adult listened to her and accepted her invitation to spend time with her. It didn't happen too often, but Mitchell never said no. Mitchell played several games with the kids until they were out of quarters and then bought them ice cream and the kids all sat in a booth together near the arcade area while Mitchell and Valerie sat towards the back alone.

Nicolette was carefully licking her vanilla ice cream cone making a game out of keeping it from being able to drip down the sides. If it dripped on her hand she would giggle and quickly lick it off her hand and get back to the game. She saw adults and her brother and sister eat the cone too but she was always too full so she just got every drop she could out of the cone before she threw it away. A lot of times her sister would eat it for her. At ten-years-old Angie seemed to have found the weight their mother lost and then some. Nicolette called her fat all the time like Angie called her stupid. Angie thought she was pretty clever when she ended the argument with at least she can fix being fat.

Nicolette was watching her mother and Mitchell at the back of the restaurant and they looked so good together. She wondered if she would get her wish and maybe Mitchell and Valerie would get married and they would all live happily ever after. Maybe it is what they were talking about at that very moment. Nicolette was overwhelmed with a feeling of love for Mitchell. She was too shy to tell him. He always held her hand and hugged her when she needed one. He told her funny stories and when she talked, he seemed to really listen to her. He was never angry and like Gerald, he was protective of Nicolette. Finally, a man she could trust.

Nicolette set her empty cone in front of her sister and stood up.

"Here fatty," she quipped.

Nicolette had decided it was time to tell Mitchell she loved him and ask him if he was going to be their new Dad. She straightened her shirt, wiped her mouth on her arm and began to approach the table where he sat with Valerie. It was hard for Nicolette to trust people and she began to get nervous to be vulnerable, but she trusted Mitchell and was going to tell him even if it scared her to death. She neared the edge of the booth where they sat and opened her mouth to speak. Just then Valerie broke her gaze with Mitchell and looked at Nicolette. Her face turned fearful and sad, pushed back from the table and rose quickly from the booth storming out of the restaurant in the rain. Mitchell looked embarrassed but it wasn't for himself. Nicolette could tell he looked guilty of something and she began to well up with anxiety. Mitchell put his hand on Nicolette's shoulder as he continued to look ashamed, but tried to be reassuring.

"I am sorry sweetheart. Did you need something? he asked.

Nicolette shrunk in her shoes and her soft face turned fearful and worried.

"No, that is okay. I don't have anything to say," she said.

Mitchell rounded the kids up, made them throw away their napkins and other trash and they joined Valerie at the van. Mitchell drove them home. Nicolette didn't feel like navigating. She just sat in a seat and stared out the window. She had always been one to have premonitions about things in life she should be too young to understand. As she watched the street lights bounce off the wet pavement and the other cars on the road she got a strange feeling she was never going to see Mitchell again and he was never going to be her Dad.

Gerald and Angie were arguing about something Nicolette didn't care about. Valerie and Mitchell were silent in the front of the van. Nicolette was silent on the outside but inside she was screaming and crying. There were voices flooding through her mind telling her she was ugly and stupid. As each voice in her mind hurled an accusation at her she etched in on her soul. One voice told her she doesn't deserve to be happy. Another voice told her she doesn't deserve to have a real Dad or a protector. A third said she is worthless and only deserves men in her life that make her tingle. At least when they leave her, she is glad. As they pulled up in front of her house, she noticed her Dad's car in the drive. A lump grew in her throat as their Mom opened the sliding door and rushed the kids out onto the curb. Mitchell waved from the driver seat and drove away. Nicolette was then certain it was only the good men who would abandon her in life. Maybe she would do well to steer clear of them.

Gerald and Angie raced each other to the front door. Nicolette followed closely behind her mother as she walked as slowly as possible as if she didn't want to go inside. Nicolette could feel her mother's sadness and defeat. She reached for Valerie's hand and although it felt limp, she held on tight to it so her mother wouldn't float away as they made their way through the front door.

"I love you, Mama," Nicolette told her.

"Go to bed," Valerie replied.

Nicolette let go of Valerie's hand and watched her mother shuffle her feet towards her bedroom as if she was headed to jail, not bed. Nicolette didn't see her Dad and her brother and sister were already in their bedrooms with the door closed. Nicolette changed into her pajamas, brushed her teeth and made her way to her bed and tucked herself in and cried herself to sleep...again.

Nicolette's head flew off of her pillow in a panic as the lamp smashed against the living room wall. It was still night time but she didn't know exactly how long she had been asleep. There were angry voices screaming from down the hall. It was her parents. She sat frozen in her bed. Terrified to move she listened closely trying to hear what their voices were saying.

"Did you sleep with him?" Stan asked.

"None of your business! Why do you care anyway?" Valerie replied.

"You slut! Do you think you can survive on a part-time job at a steak house with your boyfriend? You need me, "he said.

"I have never needed you. I am stuck with you. I would already be gone if I hadn't gotten pregnant again and you know it," she said.

"Fuck you, you bitch. Have it your way. Enjoy your boyfriend and your kids. Although he will leave you just like me. Have a nice life!" he said.

Nicolette heard the front door slam shut.

Valerie screamed one last thing as loud as she could through the front door as she pressed her back against the wall and slid down to the floor sobbing.

"He already did! He got a job in Pennsylvania you jerk!" she said.

Nicolette felt like the whole house just fell on her. She slunk down under her covers crying and felt as if she couldn't breathe. She was right, and the voices were too.

Chapter Three

From then on Valerie took frequent naps on the couch during the day before she went to work. The coffee table was ridden with dirty ashtrays full of cigarette butts and half-empty Pepsi cans. It had been a while since Nicolette had seen her mother eat and she got thinner and thinner. She eventually picked up a second waitressing job and wasn't home during the day either anymore. Gerald and Angie went to stay with their Dad in his apartment downtown up high on the eighth floor. There was always food there, unlike at home; alcohol too. Since Stan was never home it was like having their own place. The perfect set up for two teenagers wanting their independence. They could deal with Stan's angry outbursts. Gerald called Nicolette a couple of times a week, but the call always seemed vapid and rushed. It always sounded like a party was going on behind him. She didn't really want to talk to Angie or their Dad.

Nicolette felt like everything was all her fault. It wasn't her mother's fault Nicolette was cursed and would drive good men away. Her mother would have to realize only the angry men, the men who belittle her and touch her in private are the only ones who will ever stay. Mitchell left because of her and her curse. She knew it. Nicolette took over the cooking and the cleaning. By eleven she was pretty good at it. She also strictly only called Valarie Mom. It was the least she could do for ruining her life.

Nicolette finally decided it was time to visit her Dad. She was finishing up the rest of the dishes she dirtied from making her lunch when she heard him pull up in the driveway and honk the horn. She hurried outside towards the shiny blue Buick in the driveway and got it the car. It felt awkward to see him again. He was still handsome. He also still looked angry. She sat quietly on the passenger side of the car, studied the fancy dashboard, and ran her hand along with the stitching on the white vinyl seat, tracing the pattern with her finger.

Her father reached over and put his hand on her thigh.

"You look just like your mother, "he said.

Nicolette froze for a moment. It was anxiety she remembered. Her memories from childhood had faded in power and it was hard for her to remember if he had ever touched her like that before. She struggled to think if Stan had ever tried to make her tingle when she was small. His hand rubbed back and forth, then patted her leg and pulled it back. She was instantly relieved. Although it felt odd when her Dad touched her like that, she had no memories of him ever being inappropriate with her. On the rest of the drive downtown, Nicolette searched her memories. Surely it had always been friends of her parents or Uncle Felix, but never her father.

One time when her parents were still trying to make their marriage work, they went away on a trip alone together and left the kids with some friends of theirs named Mel and Tonya. Tonya couldn't have children of her own and she loved it when they got a chance to babysit. Nicolette was Tonya's favorite because she was sassy and strong like herself. Nicolette was Mel's favorite too. Mel was fun. For that visit, he had built a huge remote-control motorcycle track in an empty bedroom at his house. It glowed in the dark. He and the kids shut the door, turned out the lights and raced the cycles until dinner. When Nicolette won, he would congratulate her with a peck on the cheek or a pat on her bottom that lingered a bit. She preferred the pat on the bottom. His lips were large and wet all of the time. Although, once she thought she even felt him squeeze a bit when he patted her.

Tonya called to them when the spaghetti was ready, the lights came on and as usual, Gerald raced "Fatty" to the food trough. Before they left the room, Mel told Nicolette what a great racer she was and leaned down to peck her on the cheek. His lips slipped and he accidentally kissed her on the mouth. His wet lips were large on her face and his saliva grossed her out. Although she was confused, she thought she felt his tongue touch her lip. It was the first time an adult kissed her on the lips. It was only the second time she had ever been kissed on the lips at all. She once kissed her best friend Johnny during hide-and-seek when they were huddling together in his bathtub behind a shower curtain. They had seen it on tv and agreed to try it. After a quick peck, they wrinkled their noses, wiped it off on their sleeve, went back to the game and never tried it again. This was totally different. It was the first time she felt the tingle between her legs without being touched there.

Mel nervously brushed it off as an accident and led Nicolette to the dinner table. They all ate spaghetti together. It was good. Tonya was a great cook. Nicolette just wasn't very hungry. She took a few bites and put her fork down. Historically that was the moment the standoff with adults began over whether or not she was going to finish everything on her plate. As usual, they underestimated her stubbornness and the feud ended with her being sent to bed straight from the dinner table. It was a fate she lived over and over after dinner. Maybe one of the reasons she equates food with loneliness.

Nicolette brushed her teeth and went to the bedroom she was staying in to change into her pajamas. Tonya made sure Nicolette got the best guest room. It had one of those cool beds with the canopy and sheer curtains that hung down to the floor. It made Nicolette feel like an Indian princess or royalty of some kind. She liked that. The closet doors were two large and completely mirrored sliding doors. As Nicolette changed, she could hear her brother and sister making noise in the hall as they argued while they brushed their teeth. Once Nicolette tucked herself into bed, she heard doors close and the arguing stop. Tonya stuck her head in the door to say goodnight, smiled warmly, turned out the light and then closed the door.

Even at eleven, Nicolette had trouble remembering the complete details of that night. She just remembers falling asleep looking at the ballerina twirling on the night light cover beside her bed. The next memories are more like snapshots strung together out of order and so incoherent she was never really certain if they were bits of a dream or real memories. As she stared out the car window the snapshots flashed through her head. Mel sitting on the side of her bed naked. Mel's hand on her chest shaking her slightly to wake her. Mel's big wet lips pressed to her mouth. Mel's tongue in her mouth. Mel pulling her tiny hand down resting it on his stiff penis as she pulled it away. Her covers pulled back and her nightgown up over her head so she couldn't see. Her panties down to her ankles. The shocking memory of feeling those same unmistakable large wet lips where her panties used to be.

As she remembered the tingle, she shook her head back and forth almost violently to shake the image away. It was a trick she had developed to try and forget things. She calls it the "Etch-a-Sketch trick". Nicolette was embarrassed and began to turn red in the face when she admitted to herself the memories still made her tingle. She darted her gaze towards her Dad in the driver's seat to see if he noticed. He didn't.

Nicolette looked back out the window with her shoulders shrugged trembling, clenching her thighs tightly together and hugging herself as the car pulled into the parking lot of the eight-story apartment building. It looked different than she had pictured in her imagination. Part of her was frustrated for giving in after all this time and agreeing to visit this place, but her Dad had met a woman and moved her in. Maybe it would be better than their home was when he lived there. Maybe better than it is now without him. Nicolette would have to stay in Angie's room with her while she was there, but she would get to spend time with her brother so hopefully, the trade-off would be worth it. Nicolette had learned to travel light. Just a backpack with a change of clothes, pajamas and her toothbrush and toothpaste. That seemed to be all she needed most days.

Even at home, she had learned not to need too much. Her room was a clear indication of the change. The Winnie the Pooh décor turned to solid colors. The art hung by tacks and tape had fallen from the walls, the books were outdated and the music non-existent. The small suitcase record player and all of her storybook vinyl, as well as other toys and trinkets, were sold cheap at a garage sale her mother had last summer. When she wasn't taking care of her mother, she was doing chores, sleeping or doing homework. Nicolette wasn't a very good student. She was very smart, but her brain dealt with so many personal issues, she didn't have time to show anyone by completing her work. Assigned reading in school put her to sleep. The school was the one place she was starting to find an escape. Maybe her Dad's new place would be another.

As Stan unlocked the door to his apartment and swung it open, Nicolette was surprised how empty it was. The living room was large, the white walls were bare and the only furniture was a large leather sectional couch with the flip-up recliner ends, and two lounge chairs separated by a round table with a lamp on top. The carpet was a strange light blue color with noticeable stains from God knows what. It looked like it hadn't been vacuumed once in the few years her father lived there. The round table even had an inch of dust only disturbed by rings from what seemed to be a can of soda or beer. Just like at home, there were a couple of ashtrays full of butts and ashes. There were no pictures on the walls. No memories there. Nicolette was hoping Gerald would be there, but if he was, he certainly didn't greet them at the door.

"Well, I guess you are staying in Angie's room. Let me show you where it is," Stan said.

Nicolette followed him past the kitchen and down the hall. She was surprised how much room an eight-story apartment in the city actually had. It was about the same as their family home minus the basement of course. Stan stopped at the door with a sign on it that said, "Angie's Room Keep Out," scribbled in marker on construction paper as if she was angry when she wrote it. Angie always used to want people in her room. At home, whenever they had visitors, she tried to give everyone a tour of her bedroom to show them the new way she displayed her hairbrushes on her nightstand perfectly, the new outfits on her dolls, or how wonderfully she had straightened the shams on her bed that day. A real snore-fest. Nicolette wondered what could possibly be in a room Angie didn't want anyone to see.

"Well I will leave you to get settled," Stan said.

"Ok Dad, thanks," she replied.

She rolled her eyes as she entered the room and she was startled by what she saw. The double bed was unmade. She guessed that her and "Fatty" were going to be stuck sharing it at night time and the thought made her cringe. If she still was capable of crying herself to sleep at night, that night it would have happened. There were posters on the walls depicting the likenesses of rock bands, the ceiling was a quarter of the way covered with bottle caps pressed into the popcorn texture. From where Nicolette stood, they looked like they were from beer bottles. There were two-night stands and a tall six drawer dresser with a few drawers partly opened and clothing hanging out of them, and the surfaces of all three were covered in worn and torn teen magazines, empty soda cans and full ashtrays. Nicolette put her backpack on the rocking chair which used to hold Angie's precious dolls. Now it just had a couple of crumpled up pieces of clothing Angie must have worn at some point and some dust. Nicolette shoved them off onto the floor with the rest of the dirty clothes strewn about when she put her pack down.

Nicolette turned to re-enter the hallway and look around the rest of the place. She passed a bathroom door, another closed door, a door at the end that looked like a closet, and across from the closed-door there was an open one. Nicolette carefully crept to the doorway, grabbed the door frame, and rested her cheek against it peering around the room as if she didn't think she was supposed to go in there. Nicolette figured it must be Stan's room. There was a King-sized unmade bed, a couple of nightstands. As her eyes made their way around the room, she noticed a lounge chair and table below the window. A beautiful petite blond woman with her hair pinned up neatly sat elegantly in a pale flowing nightgown with her feet up on a footstool. She was holding a lit smoking cigarette and reading a book. Nicolette tried to read the title on the outside cover of the book hoping for a little insight on this woman's interests and if she thought she might trust her.

As Nicolette struggled to make out the title the woman lifted her gaze to meet hers and they were both visibly startled by it. The woman came to life, stood up, setting down the book but not the cigarette. She smiled wide and made sweeping grand movements with her arms as if she had just encountered royalty. A little over the top for Nicolette, but at least she didn't throw the book at her or something equally as bad.

"You must be Nicolette. I have heard so much about you. You do look just like your mother. Come in and give me a hug. So nice to meet you," she carried on.

Nicolette smiled an awkward smile unsure if she could believe the excitement in the woman's greeting, but did as she was instructed and entered the room.

She assumed this must be Margaret, her Dad's new, whatever she is.

"I am Margaret. A friend of your Dad's," she said.

Nicolette smiled. Her mild amusement turned a bit tense when Margaret flung her arms around Nicolette's shoulders and squeezed her. Nicolette realized it had actually been a while since anyone had hugged her. Besides her best friend Lynnette that is. Although she remained skeptical in lieu of further experience with her, Nicolette felt a small piece of herself immediately warm up to Margaret.

Without waiting for any response from Nicolette, Margaret whisked her off to the kitchen. It wasn't any cleaner than the living room or the bedrooms had been.

"You must be hungry," Margaret said.

Nicolette forced a smile and mumbled through her clenched teeth.

"Here we go," she said.

"What dear?" Margaret replied.

"Oh, I mean no thank you, I am full. I ate just before I came over," she said.

Margaret removed some old scattered newspapers and dirty dishes from the big oval kitchen table and put them on one of the six chairs. She put her arm down on the table and swiped some crumbs and dust off onto the floor with her sleeve, pulled back a chair, and motioned for Nicolette to sit down.

"Have a seat. I will make some coffee. I want to hear everything about you Nicolette," she said.

Nicolette could feel her throat closing on her and anxiety welled up in her body. She tried to hide the immediate reaction to hug herself while red blotches popped up first on her chest and then flared up her neck to her cheeks. She wanted to say nothing and turn around and run.

"No thank you. No offense but I am kind of tired. It has been a long day already. Would you mind if I just went and took a nap?" she said.

"Not at all, dear. That is perfectly fine. Get some rest. We have plenty of time to talk later," Margaret replied.

Margaret grabbed an open pack of cigarettes, popped one in her mouth and struggled to ignite the lighter before it sparked. She sucked on the cigarette, inhaled deep, and blew the plume up into the air towards the ceiling. Nicolette fidgeted a bit, smiled, and left the room quietly. As she approached Angie's room she glanced over at the other closed door down the hall and assumed it must be Gerald's. She walked up to it, put her hand on the doorknob and pressed her ear to the door as if trying to hear a private conversation inside. It was silent. Her thoughts drifted to memories of she and her brother sledding in the snow, riding go-carts, coloring football helmets at the table, and playing tabletop sports on the vibrating game board. She was about to turn the knob when panic overcame her. Maybe she would learn too much about who Gerald had grown into like she did when she entered Angie's room, she thought. She pushed away from the door and let go of the handle, walked into Angie's room, and closed the door behind her.

Chapter Four

Nicolette had fallen asleep on top of Angie's unmade bed and dirty clothes still fully dressed down to her shoes and hoodie as when she had arrived at Stan's place. She was startled awake by a slamming door and voices bickering and laughing. She could tell the voices were coming closer to Angie's bedroom door and she suddenly became nervous about what she assumed was going to be a long-overdue meeting between her and her siblings. With both hands, she pushed her upper body off of the pillow, a little bit of drool still on her lip and chin from sleeping so hard. Disoriented, she tried to sit up as the bedroom door flung open and a wild-looking girl with purple and pink streaks in her ponytail and piercings in her ears and nose greeted her.

"Well, how do you like that? Hi stupid, "Angie said.

Nicolette struggled to connect her memories of Angie to the face she was looking at. She recognized the eyes and the part of Angie's hair that wasn't dyed with what looked like food coloring or some other awful chemical, but this girl wasn't fat. This girl was taller and womanlier than Nicolette could comprehend. Nicolette tried to do the math in her head on how old Angie was. She looked worn and almost like an adult. If Nicolette was eleven, Angie must be only thirteen. No way, she thought.

Angie threw her purse down on the floor next to the rocking chair and jumped on the bed next to Nicolette. Nicolette had made it to the sitting position, but still stunned, moving slowly, and wiped her mouth with the sleeve of her hoodie leaving a wet spot on the light grey fabric. Angie let out a boisterous laugh.

"So, we are roommates for the night huh? Just my luck. Hope you are ready to party," she said.

Nicolette just looked at her confused and nodded her head. She wasn't really sure what Angie meant by the word party, but she figured it wouldn't be anything she really wanted to deal with. Regardless of her reservations, she didn't want to look stupid.

"Sure, why not," she replied.

"Well get yourself changed. You can't go dressed like that! If you need something to wear look through my stuff. If you can fit it in that is. Fatty," Angie said.

Angie cackled and quickly hopped off the bed and darted out the door.

"You got fifteen minutes until we are leaving," she yelled from the hallway.

Nicolette wasn't sure what she was in for, but even if she had to hang out with Angie for the evening, it couldn't be any worse than being trapped at the kitchen table with Margaret prying into her life with unending questions and hopes of bonding with her. Nicolette knew the tattered t-shirt and jeans she had thrown in her backpack probably wasn't going to be good for whatever she had in store so she got up off of the bed and rummaged through Angie's drawers and closet. Part of her was just curious about what was in there. It was clear Angie had collected a lot of clothing over the last couple of years. She wondered where she got it. Nicolette's closet at home had old t-shirts, flannel shirts, some worn jeans her mother picked up for her at the Goodwill, and way to the side smashed against the wall, hung her favorite Winnie-the-Pooh dress from when she was little. Obviously, she couldn't fit in it anymore, but it was one of the few things she salvaged before Valerie's big garage sale. It held some good memories and some bad, but it reminded her of how she loved to twirl in it and that made her smile. If she bothered to wear dresses anymore, they would have to twirl.

Nicolette's thoughts were interrupted when Angie came barging back into the room. Once Angie noticed Nicolette hadn't changed yet, Angie swiftly approached her closet, pushed Nicolette aside and started rummaging inside for something.

"Here let me help you. I don't want you to look as stupid as you actually are when the guys pick us up," Angie said.

Angie shoved a purple shirt and a short black skirt onto Nicolette's chest. Nicolette grabbed both items, rolled her eyes and turned away to inspect them as Angie walked out of the bedroom and closed the door behind her.

"Put it on and Hurry up about it, the guys are probably downstairs already!" Angie said.

"Okay get out!" Nicolette replied.

Nicolette removed her jeans and existing upper garments. She watched herself in Angie's full-length mirror unanchored and tilted against the wall. As she pulled the shimmery purple shirt over her head and situated it around her, she liked what she saw; she felt grownup. For a moment the irony of how her shirt now matched her panties she was wearing struck her. They were a white cotton bikini brief with a purple outline of lips and the purple stitched word "Kiss."

Nicolette quickly moved past that amusing coincidence and pulled the black miniskirt on past her thighs and twisted it back and forth until she thought it matched her waist correctly. Instinctively she spun in a circle. Of course, the skirt was way too snug to twirl, but she decided since it was technically a miniskirt and not a dress, she would let it slide. After a few poses in the full-length mirror, Nicolette walked over to her sister's dresser, grabbed a brush and a ponytail holder and pulled her hair up. She giggled as she thought it matched her sister's hair without the crappy chemical colors in it. As she combed her hair with her fingers, she heard Angie yell from the other room.

"Nicolette let's go!" she said.

"Coming!" she replied.

Nicolette didn't have anything to wear except her black sneakers so she just left those on. She felt a bit awkward, but that was normal for her and she was beginning to be unable to determine when she should change her behavior because of it. So, she walked out the bedroom door into the living room to make her debut. The whole room became silent as everyone turned to look in her direction. She glanced around at the faces in her new surroundings. Margaret sat with wild approving eyes. Stan looked at her and then looked away and then down at his can of beer while he spun it in his fingers. The next eyes that met hers were the ones she had been searching for since she got into Stan's car that afternoon; Gerald's. He was sitting back in one of the recliners looking half asleep. When Nicolette walked into the room, he opened his eyes wide, closed the footrest on the chair and stood up. His tired lifeless eyes beamed with new life.

"Nicolette!" he said.

"Hi Gerald," she replied.

Gerald walked swiftly across the room and hugged his sister tightly. Nicolette felt relieved, safe, and loved all within a split-second.

"Where are you two going?" Gerald asked.

"None of your business," Angie replied.

"I don't know, but do you think you will be up when we get back?" Nicolette asked.

"I will make a point of it," he responded.

Angie grabbed Nicolette's hand and dragged her out of the front door, down the elevator and into the lobby where two seemingly annoyed boys trying to be men were waiting for them.

When the two girls stepped out of the elevator Angie turned to Nicolette, reached into her purse for a tube of bright pink lipstick and grabbed Nicolette's chin.

"Hold still and pucker," she said.

Nicolette never wore makeup. When she and Angie were small, Angie used to occasionally convince Nicolette to play dress-up with her and they would sneak some of Valerie's makeup from a drawer in the bathroom and pretend they were movie stars. Nicolette didn't really have any use for it since then. Angie brushed Nicolette's cheeks with a quick stroke of blush and made her hold still long enough to apply some mascara to her eyelashes. The brush poked Nicolette in the eye and she shoved Angie's hands away from her.

"Ok, that is enough!" Nicolette snapped.

"Fine, sorry, and Joe is mine," Angie said.

Angie took off across the lobby towards the boys. Nicolette rolled her eyes, stood awkwardly for a moment, took a deep breath and began to approach the group. She could tell which one was Joe by the way Angie flung her arms around his neck and stuck her tongue in his mouth. He had bright blonde hair like Angie and blue eyes. He was dressed in a concert t-shirt and jeans. Not a very sharp dresser, but he was handsome and ripped with muscle tone. The other boy was a little taller and thinner with not as many muscles but Nicolette had to admit her heart skipped a beat when she noticed his dark tussled slightly curly hair. As she got nearer to him, his brown eyes widened and she could tell he liked what he saw. By this time Angie and Joe had exited the building into the parking lot. In anticipation of speaking to

Nicolette, the boy fidgeted and cleared his throat loudly.

"Hi," Nicolette said.

"Hi. I am Paul," he replied.

"Nice to meet you," she said.

"Nice to meet you," he said.

Paul reached for Nicolette's hand and she quickly pulled it back and went to put both hands in the back pockets of her jeans. She quickly remembered she was wearing a skirt with no pockets. Her hands floated awkwardly around her backside and back to the front. She settled on crossing her arms. She was certain she made an awkward face and felt her neck and face get really warm, hoping she wasn't getting red blotches or hives like she often does. Paul appeared a little bit startled by her actions, but he just cleared his throat again, motioned to the door, and followed her outside.

Paul led Nicolette to an older blue four-door car and as they got closer, she could see Joe in the driver's seat and Angie pressed up against him in the center with his arm around her. They were still lip-locked and Nicolette was quickly regretting agreeing to come. Paul opened the back door for Nicolette and she thought that was strange. He was acting like they were on a date and she wondered if Angie had told him something, she didn't tell Nicolette. As she slid across the vinyl bench seat, Joe started the engine and put it into drive. He started moving forward and laughed before Paul was all the way in the door. Paul slammed the door just barely missing his ankle and yelled at Joe.

"Asshole," he said.

Joe just continued to laugh and Angie joined in. Paul nervously looked at Nicolette in embarrassment and once their eyes met, they both laughed too. Paul had an attractive smile, the beginnings of a sparse pencil-thin mustache coming in on his lip. He smelled good too. Nicolette could tell Paul was at least a few years older than her but not as old as Joe who looked the same age as her brother Gerald. Paul moved closer to her and put his hand next to Nicolette's leg on the seat. She clasped her hands together and outstretched them on her legs to be careful not to bump his hand with hers and they didn't say anything else to each other the rest of the drive. Angie and Joe had lit up cigarettes in the front seat and only cracked the window open slightly so the car quickly filled with smoke.

Nicolette never had the notion to try cigarettes before even though they were always around her. She was sensitive to the smoke but never told anyone it bothered her. After all, she had grown up with it all her life. She learned it was just the way things were when the smoke stole her air and made her feel dizzy. She just brushed it off and got through it.

The car slowed to the curb of a two-story house. It was white with dark shudders and the entrance was a covered porch with a porch swing. The yard wasn't very big but there were several cars that filled the driveway and some were parked on the front lawn. The street was clogged with cars as well. There was a large group of people huddled on the porch. Nicolette could see the plumes of smoke and the orange lit ends of cigarettes in peoples' hands waving around as they chattered with each other.

Angie and Joe were already out of the car and up to the house greeting people and bantering with them. Paul held the car door open while Nicolette slid forward to the curb and to her feet. They both simultaneously looked at her black sneakers.

"They were the only shoes I had. I didn't know I would be going anywhere tonight," she said.

"That's okay I like them," Paul said.

"Thanks," she replied.

Nicolette smiled at Paul. She was starting to warm up to his kindness and seemingly gentle nature. She had resorted to the fact that he was only one of three people at the party she even knew the name of, so she might as well relax a little. While Paul closed the car door Nicolette tugged down on her skirt making sure it was covering her correctly. Paul reached out his hand again and this time Nicolette took it. His hand was soft but strong and as he led her forward, his long fingers intertwined with hers and he firmly held on to her. She liked it. It made her not feel as scared to meet all of these rowdy looking strangers. Maybe this would be more fun than she had originally thought.

Nicolette was nervous as she waded through groups of people in the house. The guys looked her up and down like she was pretty used to and the girls glared at her without missing a beat of whatever they were saying to the person facing them. Nicolette just shrugged it all off as Paul led her to the kitchen where the keg sat in a large bin of ice. He let go of her hand to fill up some cups. There were stacks of dirty cups strewn about the counters with the crumbs and ashes. There were half-empty beer bottles with used cigarette butts shoved into them. She would have sworn everyone there was smoking. The air was so thick she was trying to hide the fact she couldn't breathe well. Her head started to get woozy and the room spun a little bit and down she went.

When she came to, she was sitting on the front porch swing. Paul was sitting next to her waving a magazine near her face to fan it. Her cheek was resting against his chest and she could feel his arm around her holding her up. Nicolette put a hand on his stomach and lifted herself away from him. At the same time, she noticed, his face stricken with worry that turned calmer as she became more alert and also how good his body felt. That idea made her smile slightly. When she smiled Paul smiled back.

"Are you okay?" he asked.

"Yeah, I think the smoke was just too much for me or something," she replied.

"I was pouring us some beers and next thing I knew you were on the floor," he said.

Nicolette reached up and put her hand on her forehead; It was pounding. She felt a bump and without being able to see it she imagined it felt bigger than it probably was.

"Is it bad?" she asked.

"You definitely have a bump but you are still beautiful," he said.

They both laughed a little and then moved towards each other. Paul pressed his soft lips to Nicolette's, their mouths opened slightly and she felt his tongue touch hers. It was warm and comforting, not sloppy and wet. At that moment Nicolette let down all her barriers with Paul and put her head back on his chest as he held her tight in the porch swing.

"Do you know where the bathroom is?" Nicolette asked.

"It is inside the front door and up the stairs to the right. First door at the top of the stairs," he replied.

"Ok I will be right back," she said.

Nicolette entered the front door and closed it behind her. Joe was talking to some boys at the foot of the stairs but she had no idea where Angie was. As she approached the first step Joe asked her what she was doing. She told him and he offered to show her where the bathroom was. She nodded and he led her up the stairs, stopped at the first door and pointed.

Nicolette smiled at him and thanked him and walked into the bathroom doorway leaning towards the mirror to look at the now bruising bump on her forehead. She thought Joe had turned to go back downstairs, but he hadn't. Joe pushed his way into the bathroom and closed the door behind him locking it.

"That is some goose egg you have there Nicole," he said.

"It is Nicolette, thank you," she said.

"Come on Nicole don't be so rigid. Why aren't you more like your sister?" he asked.

He moved closer to her, turned her around inspecting her forehead more closely. Joe grabbed Nicolette around the waist and pulled her closer to him. His wet sloppy lips smelled like smoke as he started kissing her. She clenched her teeth together and tightened her lips so he couldn't stick his tongue in her mouth. He moved his lips to her neck. By now his hands were on her hips and sliding the hem of her skirt upward. His fingers slipped under her panties and rubbed her so fast she couldn't keep track of what was actually happening. Nicolette began to panic and froze. She wanted to call out, but the party was so loud they probably wouldn't hear her anyway. If they did hear her Angie would be devastated when she found out what Joe was doing. Nicolette said nothing.

Joe continued to run his hands all along Nicolette's body, pulled her panties down to her black sneakers and spun her around pushing her towards the bathroom vanity. Nicolette put both of her palms flat on the vanity and braced herself for what she knew from experience was about to happen. It was as if a switch was flipped and she floated outside of her body watching down from the ceiling. Joe unbuttoned his jeans and dropped them to the floor, he kissed her back, bottom, and thighs on the way down and then back up to a standing position. Nicolette felt him enter her hard; he was large and rough and at first, she resisted and then her body began to slowly and uncontrollably respond in slight enjoyment which conflicted her. She began moving back towards him so he would push further inside her. It only took a couple of times doing that before Joe tensed and leaned forward against her and moaned. She could feel the wetness he left as he backed away from her, pulled up his pants, smiled and walked towards the door. Joe opened the door looked back at her and said something she would never forget before he left.

"People would pay way more for you than they do your sister," he said.

Nicolette felt a sense of horror. So many questions swirled in her head. Pay her sister to do what? To do what Joe just did to her? Is that how Angie got all of the clothes? It all started to make sense to her as she pulled her clothes back on and while she cried in the mirror. Looking at herself in disbelief of what had happened her thoughts turned to Paul. Paul hangs out with Joe. Paul must know. Nicolette wiped her tears and anger swelled inside her. Why did Paul make her like him? He seemed so kind. Nicolette stormed out of the bathroom and down the stairs. All eyes were on her and she wondered if it was the bump on her forehead, her visible anger welling up inside or if they all somehow knew what had just happened upstairs. She went out to the porch where Paul sat waiting with two plastic cups of beer in his hands. One was half empty and when he saw her, he outstretched the other cup towards her. Nicolette slapped the beer out of his hand and it splashed all over the porch railing down to the ground. Paul stood up confused.

"Take me back to my Dad's!" she said.

Nicolette didn't wait for a response. She stomped to the car, slid into the backseat and slammed the car door. Paul scrambled inside the house to find Angie and Joe. After a few moments, they all appeared on the porch and started towards the car. Paul still looked confused, Joe looked angry and Angie stumbled as if unaware of her surroundings almost as if she was on some kind of drug. The way she looked it couldn't just be from beer. The three of them joined Nicolette in the car, no one said a word and they drove quietly across town back to Stan's house. The boys dropped the girls off at the apartment building and they made their way upstairs. Angie went straight to her room and collapsed on the bed. Nicolette looked around for Gerald and found him sitting in the kitchen.

"What the hell happened to you?" Gerald asked.

"Can you get Dad's keys and just drive me home?" she asked.

"Sure, no problem. Are you okay?" he asked.

"No," she said.

Nicolette left the kitchen and went into her sister's room. She changed back into the clothes she was wearing earlier that day and left the ones she borrowed from Angie on the floor next to the closet, grabbed her backpack and took a quick glance back at Angie passed out on the bed. Nicolette closed the door and met Gerald, who was waiting with the car keys in his hand by the front door. They didn't say anything to each other as they left Stan's apartment.

Once downstairs and into Stan's car Gerald started the engine, adjusted the mirrors and turned off the radio that was still on the old country station from when Nicolette arrived there earlier that day with their Dad. Nicolette fastened her seat belt. She sat there watching Gerald. He didn't have the same demeanor he used to have. He was much less talkative. Nicolette could tell he was truly happy to see her, but now that they were alone, he seemed distant. Once Gerald got everything adjusted to his comfort, he backed out of the parking space and headed towards the road. Nicolette remained quiet mulling over the events of the day since Stan picked her up. For once, going home to Valerie's house sounded safe to her. She couldn't wait to get into her old room, with some of her old things and cry herself to sleep alone like she had done since she was a child. To anyone else, this comfort would sound very strange.

"Nicolette it was really good to see you today," Gerald said.

"You too," she replied.

Nicolette started to well up with emotion inside in hopes Gerald was going to inquire about what happened that night or what had happened for the years they had been apart. It would finally be her moment to tell him the things from her early childhood. He was the one person she knew who would protect her from the predatory harm others subjected to her over the years. Once they had a conversation, he would protect her, and it would all go away.

"I have some great news," he said.

Nicolette was a bit taken back by the difference in his tone and the way she was feeling inside. Suddenly she recoiled as she realized he must not have picked up on her mood like he seemed to have earlier.

"I am getting married," he said.

Nicolette was totally taken aback. Gerald seemed happy to see her. He seemed to be the only one to notice when something was wrong when she came back to Stan's apartment. He was always the closest to her protector as she ever knew, although now as she sifted through her memories, he never really physically protected her at all. It was almost like she built him up to be what she wanted him to be because he was the closest male to her that never hurt her directly. Unless you count punching her in the arm every time, he didn't like what she said. He did it to Angie too. It wasn't personal. All three of them went through things together which no one else would understand and on the short car ride back to Angie's house Nicolette realized those times were gone.

"I want you to be at the wedding. Regina wants you to be her maid of honor," he said.

"Who is Regina? Why me? I have never even met her?" she said.

"I know, but she doesn't really have anyone else and Angie would be a distraction," he said.

Nicolette's heart sank into her stomach. She thought she was going to get to spill to her protector everything she had been through and he would somehow rescue her on his white horse and prevent anything bad from ever happening to her again. Now she realized, he just needed something from her like everyone else. It actually hurt worse than all of the other pain she had been through to date. This night was the night she knew she was totally alone. No more imaginary moments of a savior. No more holding out for that relief Gerald would bring to her suffering.

"Oh, okay sure. Does Mom know about this?" she asked.

"Well, uhm I am not sure. Actually No. Regina's parents are very strict and I am not sure how they would feel about her there. You know how Mom is," he replied.

"Yeah I do," she said.

"The thing is Regina is pregnant so her Dad is paying for the marriage," he said.

"I am sure you will be very happy. I am happy for you. Of course, I will be there. No worries. Just keep me posted," Nicolette replied.

As they pulled up to the curb outside of their old family home Nicolette felt suddenly awkward and alone. She turned to Gerald to hug him and for once in her life that felt awkward too. She opened the door and started up the walkway towards the door. Glancing back over her shoulder she saw Gerald with the interior car light still illuminated. He appeared to be waiting for her as she approached the dark doorstep fumbling for her keys. For a moment she thought she had been wrong about how little Gerald seemed to care for her now and how selfish he appeared. As she sifted through her backpack, he drove away leaving her in the shadows to find the keys by touch only. The disappointment and abandonment she felt were strangely worse than anything else she had endured up until then. She pulled the keys out of her pack, unlocked the door, entered the house, closed the door behind her and ran to her room. Nicolette didn't even wonder if her mother was home. She assumed she wasn't. She threw her backpack to her bedroom floor and threw herself down fully clothed on top of her bed and tried to cry herself to sleep just like old times. The tears didn't come but eventually, she did fall asleep.

Chapter Five

The next several years passed slowly, each day actually felt like its own year. Nicolette had become closed off to her family such as it was. She had become very thin and started most days with agonizing stomach pains. It made eating very difficult, especially breakfast. Valerie had taken her to the doctor and the diagnosis was "nervous stomach." She had some liquid acid reducers she was supposed to take three times a day, stay away from caffeine, chocolate, vitamin C, aspirin, and a few other things. Nicolette started smoking somewhere along the way at a house party with her friends, as well as a few other vices, and it helped to calm her constant anxiety.

Valerie was stuck in the same old rut. She was gone in the morning when Nicolette woke up and worked until well after the sun went down. The only way Nicolette could tell if Valerie had even been home at night was the empty beer bottles strewn about the kitchen and the ashtray full of freshly smoked cigarette butts on the table. Valerie sat in the same chair at the table every time. The seat cushion was well worn with some burn holes from stray lit ashes here and there. It smelled like a mixture of beer and coffee with the stains to match. There were stacks of coin rolls next to the placemat which was in about the same condition as the seat cushion. She would sit there on nights she was home, drink, smoke and roll the coins from her tips that day so she could deposit them in the bank a couple of times a week if they lasted that long. Sometimes she just used the coin rolls at the grocery store for a pack of cigarettes or a case of beer. Most places would accept them if she wrote her name, address and phone number clearly on the paper roll. When Nicolette was younger and her mother actually came home in the evenings, she would sit with her at the table and help her roll them. One of the only times her mother sat still long enough for Nicolette to be near to her.

Stan married Margaret and they moved out of state. Nicolette had never visited his new home. She would have to call him to have any interaction at all. She tried a few times, but quickly realized it wasn't worth the hassle. Margaret had Driven Angie out of the house with all of the constant conflict brought about by Angie's selfish attitude and actions. She bounced around living with different men for short periods of time. Nicolette heard Angie was back together with and living with Joe again. In between the other men she always seemed to end up back with Joe. Nicolette didn't get together with any extended family anymore. They seemed to enjoy Joe's presence more than her own. It was painful the couple of times she went to family gatherings with Valerie and Joe was there laughing and acting as nothing had happened between them.

Shortly after Gerald's wedding, Nicolette was playing a game of cards alone with Regina who for a while worked really hard to be close to Nicolette. It was the first time in a long time Nicolette felt like she had a real sister even though Regina was just a sister-in-law. It also allowed Nicolette to be around Gerald and their bond got strong again. Regina asked Nicolette probing questions while they played and it came out what Joe had done to her that one night. Nicolette immediately regretted it and would for years to come.

As soon as their game was finished Regina went out to the family room and told everyone Nicolette's secret. Within minutes Nicolette found herself having to explain the story over and over countless times to each family member and try to answer their intrusive questions the best she could. People made her feel like a victim and she didn't like that feeling. Once out in the open, she would have to relive the incident every time someone new found out and felt bold enough to approach her with their own questions. It was a big deal at first but eventually, the drama died down. Nicolette felt more victimized by people's comments and judgments than she did about the actual rape. Some treated her as if they didn't believe her or it was just too difficult for them to deal with the idea and didn't want to have to choose between Nicolette and Joe.

Regina's family was very religious, although they didn't always conduct themselves in a kind manner. Regina had been with countless men before she got knocked-up by Gerald. She used drugs and smoked and drank her share of alcohol. But one night she explained to Nicolette the usefulness of forgiveness. Nicolette understood the concept and had intended to get to that point where she could. Not for Joe but for herself. Nicolette was shocked and confused when the whole family decided to forgive him for her before she even had a chance to. Joe had become a permanent fixture in her family and at every function. Regina had become jealous of the time Gerald spent with Nicolette and made it clear to Nicolette she wasn't welcome to drop by their house whenever she wanted anymore. Joe had no restrictions. The family functions got harder and harder for Nicolette. She went less and less and no one seemed to notice until at some point she just stopped going at all. Her broken family was no longer hers. It was Joe's.

Nicolette's grades dropped drastically as if they really had far to go. By her Sophomore year, she was tired of wearing old shabby clothing and never having food in the house so she spent less and less time there as time went by. Most of her clothes didn't fit her anymore anyway. They hung off of her like a blanket on a wire rack. What she ate seemed the only thing she could control in her life and some days half of a candy bar was all she consumed along with massive amounts of alcohol, cigarettes and an increasing number of drugs. She met a handsome guy at a party. He was tan, strong and rippled with muscle tone and very protective of Nicolette. Her heart fluttered every time she was around him. She felt safe when he held her hand. His name was Kyle. He was a senior at an alternative school a few miles away from her. He didn't live in her area of town. Kyle had a lot of family issues of his own and a significant problem with drugs and alcohol but he was kind.

Kyle and Nicolette spent most of their time having large loud parties at an empty house in the valley Kyle had access to from a family member. Kyle truly cared for Nicolette. Aside from the wild parties and crazy nights, Kyle insisted on driving Nicolette to school every morning on his motorcycle to keep her from dropping out of school even though they were both hungover most days. Although she swooned each morning during the warm and passionate goodbye kiss, she felt desperate and lonely the moment he was gone. Nicolette hated it when she wasn't by Kyle's side. As soon as he drove away from the school to make it to his own on time, she felt empty. Her High School was very large with at least a couple of thousand students. She had hundreds of friends and acquaintances she interacted with but when she walked the halls she still felt like a ghost. Each afternoon when she was released from school she would sit on the curb and smoke a joint with a group of friends and watch the road intently and listen for the sound of Kyle's bike. She knew perfectly what the engine sounded like and could pick it out of all the other noises before she saw him round the bend.

Nicolette hadn't seen or spoken to her mother in several months. Valerie had become a nuisance showing up at high school parties thrown by Nicolette's friends in the neighborhood and on several occasions having sex with the friends' fathers. Nicolette stopped going to any parties not thrown at Kyle's house after one-night Valerie ended up at a friend's house before Nicolette arrived. Nicolette and Kyle walked in the front door hand in hand being greeted by all of their friends. As the crowd parted Nicolette saw Valerie sitting on the floor laughing and embarrassed holding a lit bong she had just tipped over onto her friend's carpet. People were booing Valerie and calling her a rookie and other disparaging names as they helped her clean it up. Valerie was wasted. Nicolette was thoroughly embarrassed and signaled to Kyle it was time to leave already. Valerie finally stopped hanging out with Nicolette's friends after she got pregnant by one of the Dads and had an abortion. Nicolette had lost the very little respect she had left for Valerie at that point.

Occasionally she would show up at Valerie's house purposefully while she wasn't there to grab a couple of pieces of clothing or other items. They would scour the cupboards and refrigerator for food or something to drink but never found much. Maybe some bar peanuts left on the table or some bologna for a sandwich if the bread wasn't moldy. But mostly beer and cigarettes and half-smoked joints they helped themselves to. There was never any mayonnaise or anything else to put on the sandwich bread. Choking it down dry was difficult but easier with a glass of tap water or sticking their face under the faucet if there weren't any clean glasses. They would get out of the house as quickly as possible to avoid the awkwardness of running into Valerie.

Everyone assumed Kyle and Nicolette would be together forever. Nicolette believed that herself. Nicolette hadn't had any intimacy with any boys since that night with Paul on the porch swing. When a boy and often grown men even looked in her direction, she would roll her eyes and scowl making sure they knew she was not interested before looking away. Kyle was the first one to make it past her defenses. He was the only one Nicolette gave her body to with permission. They didn't have sex often because of all of the drugs and alcohol but when they did, she felt loved. Nicolette often thought back to the first time they were together. It was one of her favorite memories to flit around in her head while sitting in class or oftentimes detention for too much tardiness or ISS for ditching class altogether without an excused absence.

It was the daytime. Nicolette and Kyle were riding skateboards with their friends in the empty pool in the backyard of Kyle's house while drinking Southern Comfort and Dr. Pepper. Others were smoking various things, drinking and playing games in the kitchen. Kyle planted a passionate kiss on Nicolette's lips. He was such a good kisser. Something stirred in Nicolette every time he touched her and this time, she was going to do something about it. She took Kyle's hand and led him down the hall to the master bedroom they often slept in; if they slept. She pulled off his shirt exposing his tan muscular chest and arms. His skin was always so soft and he tasted like a man as she licked him on his ear, neck and kissed his chest. He could build things and fix cars and motorcycles. The one he road he had built himself so his fingernails usually had residue on them and his nails chipped at times. His hands were so strong but also soft as he ran them down her skin from her cheek to her hips. Nicolette pulled off her shirt and unbuttoned her loose jeans. She almost didn't have to unfasten them to pull them off anymore since she was so skinny.

As she stood there in just her bra and panties Kyle was frozen looking her up and down so lovingly and his erection pressed at the front of his jeans. Nicolette had touched him a couple of times before while they were making out heavily so she knew what to expect from his bulge and she wanted to feel it inside her. Kyle approached her and removed her undergarments, laid Nicolette back on the bed as they felt each other all over, caressing, kissing, and licking each other's skin. Nicolette jumped as Kyle's fingers entered her vagina. For the first time in her life, she really enjoyed being touched and she wanted more. Nicolette rose up off of the bed, removed Kyle's jeans and as she pulled his briefs down to his thighs his manhood sprang to life. Nicolette wasn't really sure what to do next so she took a bit of extra time removing his underwear completely from his legs to think it through. She crawled on all fours back up the bed and straddled Kyle's hips. He helped position her and used a hand to guide himself into her as they both moaned in satisfaction. They moved their bodies in unison like a well-choreographed dance. With Kyle's hands firmly placed on each buttock, he pulled her forward and pushed her back on top of him faster and faster. Nicolette's back arched and her head leaned back eyes closed but towards the ceiling. She let out a breath she felt she had been holding in for so many years and she moaned loudly as an explosion of tingling sensation began deep inside her where his penis plunged. The tingle traveled down her legs to her toes. Nicolette felt it in her arms, fingers and breasts, and up to her hair follicles. It felt like finally getting to sneeze after being taunted with the sniffles. Nicolette's moan caused Kyle to immediately come inside her. He stopped moving her hips for her and held them very still as he clenched his whole body.

Even his teeth were locked together before his face relaxed, his demeanor softened, he opened his eyes and smiled at her.

When Kyle smiled at Nicolette she melted. He was the only one she allowed to look at her very long and when he did, she knew she was loved the best way anyone had ever loved her before. Nicolette was always in survival mode so she never really took the time to envision a future with Kyle. She never took the time to envision her own future while she struggled so hard to just get through each day. Nicolette and Kyle cycled in the same pattern until one day there was a knock at the front door.

By this time Nicolette had stopped going to school even though Kyle was disappointed in her. She often slept until Noon when she would get up and shower in time for him to get home from whatever odd job, he did that day. The drugs and alcohol started taking its toll and Kyle stopped showing up at his school too. His parents were furious with him for quitting so they had stopped paying the bills at the house. Kyle would get up as early as he could manage and go fix cars and motorcycles for cash so he could afford the electricity and water. The added stress changed the way they interacted. Kyle started to get mean. He had always had a temper, but not with Nicolette. Once he beat a boy to a pulp at a party for grabbing Nicolette's ass and telling her he wanted to fuck her. He usually only had to flex his muscles and threaten them to get them to leave her alone, but that boy pushed it too far. Kyle was very jealous. It wasn't until he raised his fist to her the previous night during an argument that she started thinking about their future. Thinking about how they wouldn't have one that is. Unfortunately, Nicolette felt she had no place to go.

The knocking got louder and more frequent as Nicolette slowly got out of bed squinting as the bright sun came through the broken slats on the miniblind. She pulled up her jeans and threw on one of Kyle's dirty t-shirts that were laying on the floor. The shirt hung over her tiny frame like a dress and it smelled like bike grease and alcohol with a hint of his cologne she loved. As she approached the door, she lit a cigarette and then swiped her hair out of her eyes and behind her ears, turned the knob and stood there unaffected staring blankly at the two people standing in front of her on the step.

Valerie looked cleaner, definitely not pregnant but had more flesh on her bones then Nicolette remembered. Nicolette's eyes darted towards Valerie's companion standing next to her by the door and rolled her eyes hard up into their sockets as she registered who it was. Angie's purple and pink hair was now bright blonde and her features were somehow softer. Nicolette just turned around and walked away from the open door without saying a word. She let Valerie and Angie do all of the talking and convincing. Turns out Angie had broken up with Joe again and she was now back living with Valerie for the last few months. Nicolette noticed how healthy both her mother and sister looked compared to the last time she had seen them. Valerie had stopped drinking and there was food in the house. Angie helped her clean up the house and they both worked and shared expenses. The best part was that Joe was not allowed to be there.

After about an hour of calm conversation, Nicolette felt mentally exhausted and gave in. Valerie and Angie helped Nicolette pack a garbage bag full of her things, put them in the car, and the three of them headed back to Valerie's house. Nicolette finally agreed to go with them when they promised her a burger and fries on the way there. She was suddenly very hungry and ate it like an uncultured vagabond, although she was full halfway through and couldn't finish it. Nicolette sat in the backseat while her mother and sister were in front talking and laughing. Telling stories about the fun things they had done together since Angie had moved back home. Nicolette felt like she was with strangers, but happy strangers for once. As the warmth of the sun blared through the side window and beat on her pale white skin, she felt a strange feeling she hadn't felt in a long time, if ever. Hope.

Chapter Six

Being back at Valerie's house was strange for
Nicolette. It didn't feel like her home anymore
although it felt more like an actual home more than
ever. While Nicolette was away Angie helped Valerie
fix up Nicolette's room. A man who was dating
Valerie had money and he replaced their old beds
with new ones, new appliances, and had the house
painted inside and out. Smoking was only allowed on
the back patio so the nicotine from the cigarettes
wouldn't drip down the walls on top of the new paint
as it had for years underneath. There was new
furniture in the kitchen and living room. Even new
lamps. Nicolette could still picture the old one
slamming against the wall the night her Dad left. At
the time Nicolette had left home for Kyle's house

there were still pieces of broken ceramic on the carpeting. Now the carpet was new and clean and felt comforting and soft on the bottoms of feet. Part of her didn't know how to function without chaos. Somehow, she began to feel like the blemish on the home and she took the place of the tarnished furniture and dilapidated walls. Nicolette was now the only sign of what was broken.

Kyle called several times daily for weeks. Nicolette didn't take his calls with the exception of accidentally picking it up when it rang and it was him. He didn't ask her why she left. He knew. He professed his undying love for her and explained how happy he was to finally get a hold of her. He told her his parents were forcing him into a drug treatment facility and he would be gone for three months and then returning to finish school. He wanted her to wait for him and told her he would try to call her every chance he got. She didn't have the heart to tell him she didn't love him anymore and needed to move on with her life. Partly because he was already facing enough to deal with, also because a big part of her still did. Nicolette was afraid to get swirled back up into the pattern they were stuck in. Since that sunny car ride back to Valerie's house she had begun to envision what she wanted her future to be and she didn't see Kyle in it.

"I love you, Nicolette," he said.

"I love you too Kyle," she said.

After Nicolette hung up the phone, she went to take a shower. At some point in her life, she learned the shower was the best place to cry as long as it wasn't too loud. The hot water made her whole body turn red instead of just her eyes, cheeks and anxiety blemishes on her chest. Later that afternoon she was supposed to finally meet this mystery man who had turned Valerie's and Angie's lives around. She guessed he may be the one who would turn her around too, although she had trouble believing it.

Nicolette helped Angie set the table. She had kind of forgotten how. She was really little the last time it was required. It was fun. Angie and she seemed to give each other leeway and they cracked jokes and used English accents while pretending to demonstrate setting the table at finishing school and other skits. Valerie came out of the hallway and both girls stopped in their tracks and looked at her. Valerie was so beautiful, her hair glowed, her skin was fresh, her eyes were soft and happy. She was wearing a beautiful tight fighting blouse and skirt which looked brand new. When Nicolette was small, she looked up to her mother and told everyone she was the most beautiful woman in the world and she meant it. At that moment, to Nicolette, Valerie was once again the most beautiful woman in the world.

"You look amazing Mom," Angie said.

"Yeah, you really do Mom," Nicolette said.

Valerie's eyes welled up with tears and both of the girls rushed to her side smiling trying to stop her and feeling guilty for causing it.

"That is the first time you have called me Mom in so long Nicolette," she said.

"I know. I am sorry," Nicolette replied.

"I am sorry too," Valerie said.

Valerie pulled both of her daughters' heads close to her chest and held them. They looked at each other noticing the tears in each other's eyes and smiled warmly. It was the first time Nicolette felt safe to feel love for her sister. Nicolette liked it but it made her feel uncomfortable and vulnerable.

"Ok Mom, get your boobs out of our faces," Nicolette said.

They all started to laugh while wiping tears carefully from their cheeks trying not to let their fingers disturb their makeup any more than the tears already had. Nicolette had learned to use humor to deflect the way she felt inside and to deflect intimacy with people especially when they made her feel too vulnerable. There was a strong knock on the front door and Nicolette suddenly panicked. She stood still and watched Angie and Valerie rush and play fight to get to the door first to let their visitor in. The door swung wide open and the two women stepped back to let in their dinner guest. It was Mitchell.

Nicolette instantly became a little girl again. In a split second, she relived their fun times with Mitchell and also the night he left while she cried thinking she would never see him again. Nicolette had already cried all of her tears in the shower for Kyle but her eyes managed a slight gloss and her face showed the emotion of ten thousand tears. She trembled and started to feel cold unaware Mitchell could see it from across the room. He accepted his hugs and kisses from Valerie and Angie and started towards Nicolette. Mitchell was still so handsome. He was well dressed and still had the quirky hippy look although he had gotten rid of the VW bus and long hair years ago.

"Hi, Nicolette. You are as beautiful as ever," Mitchell said.

Nicolette said nothing as Mitchell embraced her. At first, she was rigid and overwhelmed by the contact.

Once she allowed herself to relax and melt into his hug she almost collapsed into his arms. Her arms locked tighter around him than any hug she had given in years and started to cry. He petted her hair with the palm of his hand until she was able to compose herself and break the embrace to look up at his face. They both smiled wide at each other. It was the happiest feeling Nicolette had felt in years. Instantly she felt like everything was going to be alright from that day forward. Mitchell reached into his pocket, pulled out a handkerchief, and handed it to Nicolette.

"Don't cry, sweetheart. I missed you too," he said.

Nicolette was still trembling but she felt warm instead of cold. She dabbed her eyes with the kerchief, handed it back to Mitchell, and gave him another tight hug before they let go and turned to join Angie and Valerie who was across the room hugging each other watching the reunion between Mitchell and Nicolette. A few months ago they had the same scene when Mitchell came back into their lives and it made them emotional as they watched Nicolette experience the same thing.

As they ate and talked and laughed, Nicolette learned what Mitchell had been up to over the years. He had gotten a couple of prestigious degrees and had a high-profile job in some fancy law firm somewhere in New York. His restaurant days were clearly over and apparently so were Valerie's. Mitchell was moving back to town to start a private practice and at dinner, he presented Valerie with a wedding ring and asked her to marry him. Of course, she said yes. That was the smartest decision Nicolette had ever seen her mother make.

Nicolette didn't go back to school but at eighteen Mitchell convinced her to at least get her General Education Development degree. Nicolette always thought she was stupid because of her lack of focus in school and how bad her grades had been. Mitchell helped her get signed up for the GED test and drove her to the campus. He waited outside reading a book for three hours while she took it. The rules were that she takes a practice test and if she scored high enough, she wouldn't have to study and retake the main one, but it would give her an idea of the areas of study specifically important to her.

Nicolette had a lot less weighing on her mind those days so the test felt easier than she thought it would. She wasn't sure if that was a good sign or not so she was startled when the man called her name to come back to a desk and discuss her results. The last several times her name had been called to sit at a desk in a classroom setting to discuss test results it was never good news. This time surprised her and it left her welling with pride and a little stunned. She sat quietly staring at the man with her hands folded in her lap. Her leg shook nervously as he told her how well she had done. He told her she definitely didn't need to come back for the main test and they would mail her the GED completion certificate.

"I strongly urge you to go to college. Your scores are so high you are a perfect candidate for higher education. Please think about it," he said.

Nicolette was shocked. It was as if he was talking to someone else, but she was the only one sitting there in front of him. She finished listening to him speak encouraging words and thanked him as she smiled ear to ear. She had no intention of going to college. She was just getting used to thinking a couple of days or maybe a week ahead but just hearing him saying the words stirred something in her. When she walked out of the testing room and into the hallway Mitchell rose to his feet smiling and asked her how she did.

"You are not going to believe this," she said.

"Sure, I will," he said.

The two of them walked out of the school, Mitchell's arm around her shoulder. Nicolette was chattering the whole way out of the building, into the car, and almost the whole ride home. Mitchell listened quietly with expressions of joy and acceptance on his face that ignited Nicolette's energy as she continued telling her story. Nicolette loved Mitchell. He was the closest to a father she had ever had. When they were halfway home Mitchell seemed to have made a wrong turn. Nicolette quickly realized what he was doing when he pulled the car into the old ice cream place, he used to take her to when she was a kid. They enjoyed their ice cream laughing and talking across the table. When they were finished Mitchell reached across the table and took each of Nicolette's hands on his own. Nicolette started to feel nervous. She had flashbacks of when other grown men had touched her hands that way and the uncomfortable salacious words that came out of their lips.

Mitchell held her hands gently, bowed his head and began to pray.

"Father God, I thank you that you have led Nicolette to this place in her life. I thank you for showing her how intelligent, kind and beautiful she is. Please walk with her for the rest of her life and let her always know she is never alone and remind her how strong she is through you. In Jesus's name," he said.

Nicolette was stunned. She felt warm all over her body. Her anxiety was replaced with comfort as Mitchell asked her if she would like to give her life to Jesus. Nicolette used to read bible story books when she was young and sometimes, she found herself sitting cross-legged on the floor watching television preachers tell stories. She would turn it off when they asked for money because she had nothing to send anyway and felt guilty for watching if she couldn't pay. When Valerie was spiraling, she would bring her the bible and ask her mother to read to her words of parables and Psalms. Valerie did a couple of times before she didn't want to anymore. In high school, while she was in detention, she would scribble the words "Jesus saves' onto her notebooks and the bottoms of her sneakers. She didn't know why exactly.

Nicolette bowed her head and repeated the words Mitchell spoke and when they both opened their eyes, she realized Jesus had just saved her like her shoes and notebook said he could. She wasn't sure what that really meant in terms of life and what happens next, but something in her was more powerful and stronger than ever before. She felt the drive to make a better life for herself and started to daydream of the future. It was like how some mothers described being pregnant and carrying their baby. How full of life they felt and that they never felt alone with the child they created inside them. Nicolette felt pregnant with warmth, love, and ideas. For the first time in her life, she didn't feel alone.

Mitchell and Nicolette got back in the car feeling so close after what they had just shared together. It was as if Mitchell had completed the task, he was put on earth to do. He looked so proud of Nicolette. She was proud of herself. She could see herself the way Mitchell looked at her now. Nicolette hoped the rest of her life would feel this way. As they made a right turn at the last stoplight before home she glanced away from Mitchell's face and through the driver side window. A look of horror on her face as a fast-moving truck was headed directly for their car.

Nicolette awakened in a hospital room. All eyes were on her. A doctor, two nurses, Angie and Gerald. She asked them what happened. As she spoke, her voice barely came out audible and the pain in her head was immense and making her cringe as if someone else had yelled in her ear as her words came out.

"Where is Mitchell?" she asked.

Tears started to flow from Gerald's and Angie's eyes. Her mother's face appeared in her view as Valerie stood up from a chair seated next to Nicolette's bed. There were black mascara and eyeliner streaks all down her face and her eyes were so red and puffy it looked like she had been crying for days. Valerie couldn't speak, she just leaned over and kissed Nicolette on the forehead.

"I am so glad you are okay sweetheart," Valerie said.

"Where is Mitchell?" Nicolette repeated.

As she asked the question everyone looked at each other stumped as if searching their minds for an appropriate answer. The doctor took the place beside her bed where her mother had been and Valerie slumped back down in the chair sobbing. Angie rushed to hold and console her. Gerald stood frozen, his face deadpan at the foot of Nicolette's bed as the doctor explained to her that Mitchell hadn't survived the accident.

Chapter Seven

After Mitchell's death, Nicolette expected her mother to fall apart again. She also expected herself to fall apart. But Nicolette had a calm resolve about herself even when the pain was on high. Maybe it was having gone through all of the things she had endured since she was born, hell maybe even in the womb. Maybe it was the comfort of the last day she spent with Mitchell and how much she knew he genuinely loved her. Maybe it was the prayer he prayed with her that day when she pledged her life to Jesus. She had a chance to share that moment with her mother and all of the events leading up to the crash. Nicolette could see her mother was in serious pain of loss, what could have been and what would never be. Gerald and Regina brought Valerie to their church and apparently there was some kind of dramatic saving of soul that went on that day, but Nicolette wasn't there to witness it.

Valerie started reading the Bible and going to a church of her own. She quoted scripture often and seemed stronger than ever although sometimes at night Nicolette could hear her crying in the room next door and Mitchell's name was audible. Nicolette cried for him too sometimes. But strangely she carried him with her in her heart in a way no loss had ever resonated with her before. Nicolette had always lost everything she ever took the time to love. But this time she wasn't abandoned. It was an accident. She knew if he could, Mitchell would still be alive and her biggest supporter on the sidelines of her life cheering her on. Somehow, he still was.

Angie moved out and in with a man she met which was no surprise to Nicolette. They stayed cordial but distant. They never again were able to recapture the time they spent together setting tables and eating family dinners with Mitchell. It was as if being together for any of them at this point was just too painful. They had been through enough carnage as a family and there just wasn't any room for more.

Nicolette watched her mother clutch to church and scripture the same way she clutched to alcohol, chaos, drugs, men, and nicotine. The love and acceptance turned towards criticism and rebuke for any imperfect decision Nicolette made. When she turned twenty Nicolette realized she could no longer justify not living on her own making a life for herself. The words of the GED test administrator began to almost haunt her. So did Mitchell's words.

Nicolette applied for college several states away. It was just a community college she thought but it was a start. They told her if she moved to town first and lived there for six months her tuition would be about half the cost. With the money Mitchell left Valerie in his will she knew her mother could take care of herself. Mitchell left Nicolette just enough to probably afford living expenses for those six months while she found a job in a strange state and pay her first tuition expenses.

Nicolette's love of music reemerged. A new band came on the scene. One day while she sat on the sofa eating white cheddar popcorn skimming a music magazine, she saw a story on this band. It was three guys seemingly in their twenties like she was, barely. They looked nerdy and fun. Something sparked her as she saw the lead singer's face. His name was Justin

Bend. He looked rather apathetic and silly but something in his eyes connected with her even through a two-dimensional picture.

"I am going to be with him someday," she said to herself.

The thought made her laugh. Although Nicolette had proven to have a strange gift of foretelling certain incidents accurately. It was easier to be sure when it was about someone else. She never believed them outright if they pertained to her unless it later transpired or proved itself, but it did make her take note. Many times, she would get a premonition or a vision but it was sometimes poisoned by thoughts of what she wanted instead of the actual events that would unfold. Something about this man told her he would come for her but she felt she knew it was going to be sometime between forever and never, so she just went on about her life and enjoyed the music from many bands not dwelling on one face. Nicolette purchased his CD and listened to it non-stop it was so good. It spoke her language. He seemed to speak her language.

Valerie had helped Nicolette get a small compact car for the journey. It wasn't fancy, but it was reliable. It was a tearful goodbye, but both of them also seemed ready to let go. The day Nicolette packed her car and drove away from her mother's house she listened to Justin's band along the way several times as well as countless hours of other songs from her life. It was almost therapeutic and helped her unpack some of life's challenges she had encountered as she sang along. Nicolette daydreamed of what life would be like when she got to her new home. She planned to stay in a motel near the school campus and begin a search for an apartment. Thanks to Mitchell she could afford to be a little loose with her plans.

Nicolette had never branched out on her own before and she felt a certain freeness in taking such a big step outside of her comfort zone. Any time fear crept in she asked herself how worse can life get? A certain optimism lived inside her now. What used to scare her into a corner and make her cry herself to sleep or sob quietly in the shower now seemed to motivate her to push harder. After all, what did she have to lose? Stan nicknamed her "cockroach" when she was little. He said it was because he knew she could survive anything. It was way before her parents divorced and Angie and Nicolette would sit with him while he talked on the CB radio so he gave both the girl handles to go by when he let them speak on air. Angie's was "Kitten." Quite a contrast. Nicolette grew to believe he was somewhat prophetic in his naming. Maybe she could survive anything.

After several hundred miles and a few stops for gas Nicolette was hungry for more than Cheetos and fountain Coke with crushed ice. She took an exit marked with the symbols for gas, lodging, and food. As the car slowed at the top of the offramp, the gas sign had an arrow to the left and the rest to the right. Nicolette couldn't decide if she should check into the motel and then go eat or stop at the roadside diner in her view and eat first. Her stomach was making loud grumbling noises so she settled on the diner. It was a restaurant called Denny's. She has seen many scattered about along her path so far so she decided to try it. The parking lot was pretty full but she found a spot near the back of the building. She wondered for a moment if she should take her backpack or anything else with her or leave them in the car. Nicolette just grabbed her purse, locked the car, and walked around the back of the building to the front double doors.

There were people of all shapes and sizes walking in and around the front entrance. The crowd made her a little nervous but she straightened her back with her chin up and walked through them like she wasn't concerned. Nicolette walked up to the hostess podium where a young girl chewing gum was scratching off names in a book with a pen as she called them out loud. Nicolette stood there awkward shuffling her feet waiting for the hostess to return from taking four loud people to a table with menus and returned to greet Nicolette. Her nametag said, Shirley.

"The wait is about 45 minutes. Unless you want to sit at the counter, there are a couple of seats open up there. Since it is just you, I would." she said.

Nicolette nodded her head and wandered up to the counter. There were two open seats. One wedged between two big, hairy men with ballcaps and overalls talking loudly to each other across the empty seat. The other was around the counter all the way to the end by the bathrooms where the surface was a bit blocked by a glass rack and bins of silverware. The person in the seat next to that open one was a smaller middle-aged woman with glasses, drinking coffee, smoking a cigarette, and marking with a pen on what looked like a crossword puzzle. Nicolette chose to contend with the smoke instead and took her place next to the woman. The woman didn't acknowledge her at all. Perfect. A tall waitress with worn skin, too much makeup, dangly earrings, and a big warm smile swiftly greeted Nicolette while plopping a plastic multipage menu down in front of her.

"Hi, sweetie. How are you? Can I start you with something to drink? Pancakes are on special. They are always on special," she said.

Nicolette let out a chuckle. She scanned the lady's name tag which read Shelby. Her outgoing nature and obvious sense of humor immediately put Nicolette at ease. After quickly skimming the menu looking for the drink section. Shelby flipped the book over and plunked her finger down on the bottom section of the page where the drinks were.

"I will just have large chocolate milk please," she said.

"Sure Sugar, no problem. I will be right back with that," Shelby said.

Nicolette could rarely eat pancakes in the morning because of her nervous stomach. She could only drink milk around lunchtime because if she did too early in the morning it clashed with the acid in her stomach and she would feel sick the rest of the day. Shelby returned with the glass of milk, set it down, and raised her pen to her order pad while she smacked on her gum.

"What'll it be then?" she asked.

Nicolette liked Shelby the more she spoke. She was almost like an animated character right out of any movie with a diner scene and the irony was not lost on Nicolette. The places Valerie worked didn't have any bigger than life personalities. They always seemed to be disgruntled older women who hated their job and would just as soon spit in your food than be kind and make you laugh.

Nicolette settled on the two-egg breakfast with hash browns and bacon. Shelby talked her into basted eggs to dip her sourdough toast in. It was delicious. As she sat and ate her food Nicolette glanced around the room watching people eat and laugh at each other's stories. There was a round table booth in the corner with six older women playing cards and smoking while they ate. Nicolette shook her head at how disgusting that must taste.

Nicolette didn't have any use for cigarettes or alcohol after the car accident. She wanted to treat herself better and that was the first two changes she made. Her thought process was interrupted when her eyes scanned past a younger couple sitting in a booth together but far apart. The looks on their faces, body language, and the way they tried to hide their mouths while they took turns talking made Nicolette wonder if they were lovers breaking up. She had seen that scene many times and just assumed she was probably correct. Nicolette hadn't dated anyone since Kyle so she had never really been a part of one of those scenes. She wondered how Kyle was sometimes but only for fleeting moments.

Shelby took the signal when Nicolette wiped her mouth with a napkin and tossed it down on top of her plate of half-finished food. She came quickly to her end of the counter, picked up the dirty plate and threw it in a bin below out of Nicolette's sight and asked her if she could bring her anything else. Nicolette politely declined and Shelby set a paper check down in front of her, smiled and whisked off to the other end of the counter with a pot of coffee topping off people's cups. The total was just over seven dollars. Nicolette put down a ten-dollar bill, got up from her seat and made her way to the front door watching Shelby the whole way. Shelby noticed her, smiled her big smile and waved goodbye. Nicolette smiled, waved back and left the building.

Nicolette was looking around the parking lot trying to judge which lot exit would be best to take to get across the road to the motel. As she approached her vehicle it took a minute to sink in, that her back driver-side window was broken and there was glass strewn about the gravel around her car. Her feet picked up pace as she reached the car door and opened it. The glass crunched under her shoes. Her backpack was opened and her clothes pulled out onto the seat. Her makeup bag was opened but nothing was missing. The sunglasses she had on the dashboard were missing and some change from the ashtray from her stops along her travels. Her CDs were also missing.

Nicolette glanced around the parking lot looking for a glimpse of who might have done this. All she found was two of her CDs that must have been discarded or dropped laid smashed and broken in the gravel as it they had been stepped on. One of them was Justin's. Her heart sank into her stomach thinking about what kind of monster could be so shallow and unkind as to steal someone's things. Nicolette never really had too much in her life. Surely there are better things to be stolen than some loose pocket change, sunglasses, and some compact disc music. She had no idea what to do about the window.

Nicolette felt violated as she bent down and picked up the broken Justin Bend CD and the other laying in the dirt. She clutched them close to her as she looked around, got back into her car and started towards the motel. Before she went inside to ask for a room, she repacked her belongings, swept as much of the broken glass out of her car and brought everything inside with her. There was no need to lock the car with her missing window. Not like there was anything left in there to steal.

Optimism versus self-defeat was a well-known struggle Nicolette had become accustomed to. Regardless of the optimism born into her that day Mitchell prayed with her, the self-defeat ingrained in her since the beginning of her life was still there too. It wasn't as if it just left her that day. It was just forced to make room for its nemesis. When the switch flipped from dark to light it was automatic and out of her control. It controlled her. As she unlocked the door to her shabby motel room, she was exhausted. She thought about her journey so far and less about what she was journeying too. As she tucked herself into a strange bed she wondered if she had in fact

made a huge mistake.

Chapter Eight

Nicolette awakened in her motel bed when a ray of sunlight moved across the bed and settled on her face. She rubbed her eyes with the back of her hand as she sat up trying to block the glare. After a quick shower and a change of clothes, she headed downstairs for the free breakfast complimentary with a night stay. As she entered the lobby, she placed her room key on the front desk and thanked the attendant. After browsing the small room full of freshly brewed coffee, stale muffins and rancid fruit cups it occurred to her she could go back to the diner. Nicolette thought it would be fun to watch Shelby do her Shelby the diner waitress impression again before she left on the road.

After sleeping in a strange bed in a strange room not connected to a house full of rotten memories and some good, she started to feel a strange mixture of accomplishment and loneliness. As she carried her things towards her car she was approached by a man she had seen watching her across the lot. He was handsome, not much older than her and he wore a cowboy hat and tight jeans. His look stirred a slight attraction to his form. As he approached her, he removed his hat and pressed it to his chest cautiously outstretching his hand. Nicolette wasn't sure if she was supposed to shake it or just greet it with hers and let him take the lead. She outstretched her hand and he held it softly for just a moment and let go.

"Good morning Miss," he said.

"Good morning," she said.

Nicolette was a little confused by how non-intrusive this intrusion felt. The man introduced himself as Paul. Nicolette was a little taken aback by the name at first but she calmed herself and waited to hear what he had to say to her. Paul explained he saw her drive in the prior evening and noticed her car window was broken. He explained to her their town had a problem at travel areas of thefts at night. Paul also told her he had watched her car through the night and could fix it for her before she continued on to where she was going if she wanted him to. Benny's auto parts had plenty of window glass on hand and Nicolette's was a pretty standard type.

Nicolette was baffled that a total stranger would take an entire night to watch her property albeit too late to save her possessions inside the car, but none the less thankful for it. She had to admit, the thought had occurred to her she might come out in the morning and find her car completely gone.

"Wow. That would be amazing. I still have a long way to go. Thank you," she said.

"No problem Miss," he said.

"Don't call me Miss. Call me Nicolette," she said.

They smiled at each other and Nicolette trailed behind him slightly as she watched him turn to open a pickup truck door. The door had the word Sherriff written across it with a seal. She guessed he must be a deputy. The town couldn't be big enough to need two. That explained why he would stay up all night watching one car. There can't be too much else going on there. Nicolette tried to stifle her cynical thoughts of how this guy must have felt obligated to watch her car and it wasn't just a random act of kindness. She tried to remain grateful, but she was a little disappointed.

Nicolette had a knack for quickly dreaming up fairy tale scenarios that placed two people on the same path at least momentarily. It was the antidote to the nihilism that used to rule her. Paul returned to Nicolette's car with a piece of cardboard and some tape. He covered the broken window with the cardboard and taped it to the door.

"There that should keep for now until we get to the shop. Follow my truck in your car. I will drive slow," he said.

"Okay," she said.

Nicolette had a fleeting thought about how dangerous it might be to follow a complete stranger in her car to a place she had never been. She also needed her window fixed. If it was a local shop, they were going to Paul called Benny's, she would obviously know if that was where he was taking her. Surely there was a sign. After all, she was driving her own car and could turn around and head straight back to the highway at the first sign of trouble.

By the time Nicolette had convinced herself she wasn't doing anything wrong, they had arrived at Benny's. A dilapidated wooden sign stood on a sturdy wooden pole on the corner of the property. Electricity lines and phone lines hanging from other poles. A modest building with two open bay doors and a small showroom with lots of windows were attached. Nicolette parked next to Paul. He walked into the main entrance of the building as she trailed behind him slightly until they reached the door. He pulled his hat off and again pressed it to his chest and motioned for her to enter first.

Nicolette thought his actions were strange, but she liked it. Paul was very charming and kind. Her heart fluttered a little bit even though she fought it. This was just a kind stranger she would never see again after today and if he helped her fix her car and get back on the road then great. No need to attach feelings to him.

Nicolette had a way of quickly attaching feelings to people whether good or bad. It was partly her premonitions of them and the other part was her innate desire for meaningful connections. Even bad connections were meaningful but she was actively searching to have more of the good kind. She just tried not to get in the way of them without too much rigidity or she might crush anything good and only the bad would get in. She spent so much of her earlier life scared of everything so she silently vowed to try and accept the good and the bad and stay open to anything. She hoped her world might flow better that way.

Nicolette waited near the door for Paul as she watched him talk to the man behind the counter, she assumed was Benny who smiled at her briefly as he led Paul to a selection of car windows. Paul took out his small notepad and flipped up a page or two before reading Benny the information written in it. They agreed on a window and returned to the counter where she watched Paul give a credit card to pay.

Nicolette immediately got uncomfortable and shifted back and forth from foot to foot. She was certain Paul intended to pay for her window and she knew to pay for it herself would set her current plan back a little bit but she wasn't certain if she wanted to owe anyone anything. As she approached the counter to stop Paul and tell him she could afford the window herself. He simply looked at her, smiled warmly and spoke.

"Just let me do this for you. You need the help and to be honest, it helps me more than it helps you," he said.

He squinted his eyes and smiled at her warmly while he waited for a response. Nicolette was momentarily stunned by his kindness. He didn't seem to want anything in return but maybe he did. The only thing people ever seemed to want from her was her body. Maybe he wanted that in return. Oh, who knows, maybe he didn't, she thought.

"Thank you for your kindness," she said.

It was as if someone answered for her using her mouth and her voice but those weren't her words. She wanted to tell him no thank you and she couldn't be bought but something in her calmed her and made her know this was a genuine act of kindness on Paul's part.

"You are very welcome," Paul said.

Once outside Nicolette handed Paul her car keys so he could drive the car into one of the bays so Benny could replace the window. Paul asked Nicolette if she had eaten and she told him no. After some coaxing, he convinced her they should take his truck and drive back to the Denny's and have some breakfast. She agreed. He held the door for her when they exited Benny's and again at his passenger side truck door. Nicolette hesitated for a second before she threw caution to the wind and hopped up on the running board to seat herself in Paul's truck. They smiled at each other as he carefully closed the truck door, made his way around and hopped into the driver's seat.

Nicolette was now fully attracted to Paul. She was still disturbed by his name but maybe this Paul could erase the bad memories the last Paul left in her mind. Maybe that was the whole point. Something just as simple as that. She didn't know but she enjoyed watching him drive her to the diner. His jaw was strong and had a short-manicured beard but it grew in full. Nicolette noticed his eyes were green and they sparkled. His lips looked soft and for a moment she wondered what they tasted like. When Paul reached into his glove box and pulled out a can of Copenhagen and put a dip in his lip, she suddenly knew the answer, at least partly.

Nicolette reined back in her forming desires of this rugged man who had been there for her in her time of need just in time for the truck to pull in to Denny's parking lot. They went in and as the hostess sat them in a booth Nicolette noticed Shelby up behind the counter just like she was the day before. She looked more worn and had a scowl on her face. Nicolette felt they had somehow bonded with their interaction the day before but Shelby made eye contact with her and with the exception of a sharp momentary glare Shelby acted like she didn't notice or remember her. The waitress that did approach them knew Paul's name and kept glancing from Shelby to Paul as if they all knew something Nicolette didn't know and she started to get nervous. The waitress took their order short and quick and disappeared to go put it into the kitchen.

It was common for Nicolette to create a story wrapped around people's non-verbal communication. She had learned it often tells a much more accurate tale than the one that comes out of people's mouths. Was there a connection between Shelby and Paul? There was only one way to find out.

"Do you come in here often?" she asked.

"Yes, and if you wonder why that woman behind the counter is scowling at you it is because we dated for a few short months a couple of years ago and she hasn't gotten over me breaking up with her yet," he said.

Nicolette was floored that Paul knew exactly what she was really asking and just easily blurted all of the answers out for her to know. It was rare for someone to be that candid with her. He noticed the non-verbal communication in the room. They were on the same wavelength it seemed. It wasn't just Nicolette's imagination. He gave her confirmation that her intuition is good and just because people in the past who meant her harm told her it was her imagination didn't mean that was true.

Paul and Nicolette enjoyed their food and conversation. While Shelby scowled, they laughed and got to know each other as much as they could in a couple of hours anyway. After that Paul returned Nicolette to Benny's and her car was finished. Paul pulled the car out of the bay and parked it back in the lot next to his truck, got out, and handed Nicolette her keys and the receipt for the repair.

"Make sure to keep that receipt in your glove compartment in case something goes wrong," Paul said.

"I don't know how to thank you," she said.

"You already did," he said.

Nicolette was overwhelmed with gratitude and attraction for Paul. She threw her hands up and wrapped them around his neck and they enjoyed a lingering embrace. As they stepped back from one another Nicolette was overwhelmed with emotion and she lunged at Paul and pressed her lips on his. She wasn't worried about finding out what chewing tobacco tasted like anymore. He kissed her back but only for a moment before gently pushing her away.

"I helped you because you needed it not because I wanted something," he said.

Nicolette was stunned. It was a mixture of insult for the rejection and complete and total respect for Paul. It was rare for anyone to do anything kind for Nicolette without wanting something in return even if it wasn't presented that way at first as some sort of a quid pro quo. Somehow it always seemed to end up her owing and paying up or being discarded and abandoned. This Paul was different.

"You are beautiful, funny, kind and wonderful to talk to. If you lived here we could hang out with each other and likely be very good friends, but you owe me nothing," he said.

Nicolette carved a special place in her heart for this Paul that day. She leaned in and gave him another tight warm hug, let go, and waved as she got into her car and got back on the highway. As she now listened to the radio that crackled and faded in and out along the way, her thoughts were with Paul and the gift he gave to her that day.

Chapter Nine

Nicolette was getting weary on her drive and wanted to stop to rest but the sign said only sixty-eight miles left to her new home town. Her eyes were irritated by the glare from the headlights of oncoming traffic on the highway. It seemed more people were going away from where she was headed instead of towards it and wondered momentarily if that was a bad sign.

Nicolette was frustrated by the radio cutting out in the middle of songs she was singing along to so she settled on a mostly audible talk radio station. She caught the tail end of a self-proclaimed relationship expert giving advice to couples about various trivial problems. When she stopped for gas, she grabbed some questionable truck stop coffee and an apple fritter from the day-old donut cabinet. When she returned to her car the advice guru was done imparting her wisdom so for the rest of her drive, she listened to a man who talked so passionately about UFO sightings she almost believed him. He took calls from listeners with claims of their own experiences.

As the lonely two-lane highway turned into a slightly more populated multi-laned one, Nicolette started to see signs for business parks, mattress stores, and restaurants. She started to pass by residential areas and regular gas stations instead of truck stops. When she saw the sign for the Willette County Community College she felt immediate relief knowing her long road trip was coming to an end. Nicolette questioned her choice to get the apple fritter. She had crumbs all over her lap and on her car seat. Her fingers clung slightly to her steering wheel from the leftover stickiness she couldn't seem to lick off. No matter how many times she rubbed her hands on her pant legs it was still there.

Nicolette took the exit for the school so she could see what kind of area it was in and curious if there was a place for her to stay nearby. Just her luck there was a clean looking two-story motel sign glowing a block ahead of the school just past an intersection. It was in the same parking lot as someplace called the Rusty Spur Bar and Grill. This time she decided to check into her room with what was left of her belongings from her car and take a shower before wandering across the lot to get something to eat. Regardless of the low probability of getting her car broken into twice in two days, she wasn't going to take the chance. After all, it was doubtful all towns had a Paul.

The Bar had windows but they were amber in color so she could only see shadowy figures inside. The big wooden door was heavy so she had to pull with both hands to swing it open. The Hinges made a metal scraping sound followed by a squeak that lasted until it closed behind her. There was no hostess on duty, just a sign that said to sit anywhere. There were only about fifteen or twenty people there with one waitress and one bartender leaning across the bar talking to each other.

Nicolette wasn't twenty-one yet and wasn't sure if she was allowed to sit at the bar so she took a seat at a four-top table near a jukebox and a small dance floor. There was an older couple holding each other tight and swaying to the music. They didn't even seem to notice anyone else was around them. It was as if they were the only two people in the world. Part of Nicolette wanted that someday. The other part of her pictured the couple having too much to drink, going home, throwing lamps at the wall, and fighting until they passed out. She hoped that wasn't true for those two.

Nicolette was glancing over the menu when the waitress approached her. When she looked up to greet her, she noticed two guys at a nearby table drinking beer, talking loudly, and laughing at something. The waitress who took Nicolette's order wasn't wearing a nametag. She was bubbly and happy but she didn't offer her name. The woman was slender, had bright blue eyes, and almost black hair cut, sharp across the bottom in a bob style. Nicolette ordered the Chicken Caesar Salad and a cranberry juice. The waitress skipped off towards the bar to notify the kitchen as all the men in the bar watched her go. Nicolette watched the bartender fill her bar glass with straight cranberry juice from his beverage gun, toss it back in the holster, and plunk her glass up on the bar top with a small piece of paper that shot out of an order machine next to him. He glanced over at her and smiled.

The bar walls were adorned with framed photos of cowboys and cowgirls. Some famous with signatures. There were old wagon wheels and boots up high on shelves and other various western type items mounted about the place. All of the tables and chairs were heavy solid wood. There was one row of booths across the front of the building where the Amber windows decorated with iron panes were. Nicolette's attention was drawn back to the two men near her drinking beer. One of them kept staring at her as he spoke to the other and then broke gaze when she made eye contact. Nicolette could tell he was interested. He kept tapping his boot nervously on the wood floor.

He was very good looking with his big brown eyes and well-manicured goatee. He wore a cowboy hat but it was different than Paul's. It was darker and made him look more like an outlaw than a deputy. His perfectly pressed dark collared shirt was tucked into his jeans with a belt and a shiny buckle. He looked fit and his biceps bulged out of the tight fit of his short sleeves. She could see the slight markings of what looked like a tattoo peeking out of the sleeve on his left arm but couldn't tell what it was supposed to be. The other man he was talking to was clean-cut and his hair was very short with a spot on his crown beginning to bald. He wore a wrinkly collared shirt half-tucked into his jeans and sneakers instead of boots.

Nicolette was distracted from sizing up the two men when the waitress brought her the cranberry juice and slid her salad in front of her. Nicolette was so hopped up on caffeine and sugar from the drive she was a bit jittery. As she ate her food and sipped her drink she watched various people picking songs on the jukebox and dancing to them. She was never really a dancer. With the exceptions of twirling in her dresses as a young girl and once standing on Stan's boot toes as he pretended to two-step when she was really small, she had no experience. There was a school dance when she was in eighth grade, but everyone just stood around talking in groups and drinking punch. Nicolette had to wear jeans and a t-shirt because she didn't have any money for a dress like most of the girls. Only a few people really danced at all and she wasn't one of them. Dancing made her feel awkward. Since she had dropped out of school, she never had a graduation or prom and no real opportunity to learn.

The waitress returned to clear Nicolette's table. Nicolette asked her to leave the cranberry juice there because she was going to run to the restroom. Nicolette could feel cowboy hat guy's eyes on her as she stood and walked around to the side of the bar, opened the bathroom door, and went inside. Before she left the room, she pulled her hair up into a ponytail with the band she had kept around her wrist. She pulled a tube of pink lipstick out of her purse and put some on. After a few kissy faces in the mirror and a chuckle, she returned to the bar. As she came back out of the door cowboy hat guy saw her and locked his gaze on her. This time he couldn't look away. Nicolette was hoping that might happen and when it did, she smiled at him and quickly looked away from him as a tease. As she walked by his table, she could feel a magnetic heat between the two of them. He watched her closely as she sat back down at her table.

As she sipped the last of her cranberry juice, she made sure to lick the rim of the glass a couple of times while she stared right at him and he didn't miss any of it. She didn't quite know why she was doing this but she couldn't control herself. As she was looking at the amount of the check and fumbling through her purse for the correct amount to pay, cowboy hat guy was now standing next to her table looking down at her. As she raised her eyes up, she scanned his body from his boots to his jeans and up to his face. When she looked up into his eyes, she appeared innocent as a doe but the thoughts running through her mind were anything but. The look on his face told her their thoughts were very much on the same page.

"Hi, is this seat taken?" he asked.

"You have been watching me for the last hour so you know it's not," she said.

"Yes, you got me. What are you drinking? I think you need to stay for one more," he said.

"It is cranberry juice," she said.

"You are going to need something stronger than that," he said.

Instead of taking the seat across from her, he pulled a chair right beside her as close as he could get and looked directly at her as if the table wasn't there. Nicolette's heart raced from his close proximity. She stopped fumbling for her money and set her purse down because suddenly she could no longer count. If walking near his table was magnetic heat, this was a blazing fire. The waitress came back to see if they needed anything and it was obvious, she could feel their electricity emanating from the table.

"We will take two tequila shots with lime and salt," he said.

Nicolette was about to explain to him that she wasn't old enough to drink in a bar but she was cut short by the waitress's smile and wink.

"Coming right up!" she said.

Nicolette was intimidated all of a sudden. She was trying to intimidate him and felt like he just took the lead in the race. Cowboy hat guy finally introduced himself as Jamie and Nicolette shared the nickname, she had already given him. They laughed, talked, and listened to each other intently about why she was in Willette, why he was there, and what their life goals were. After several tequila shots and hours later, the bar was closing down and they knew they had to leave. Jamie walked Nicolette to the parking lot and asked her where her car was. She pointed over at the motel. His eyes perked up and he asked her if he could walk her to her room. She agreed.

He clasped his hand in hers and they started walking towards the motel. Nicolette's mind was racing. Would he just walk her to her door? Would he want to come in? Would she let him? Yes, of course, she would. She felt exhilarated and he was so sexy and good looking she hoped he wanted to stay with her. She wanted to know what he looked like without his shirt and curious to know what his tattoo said. He looked so good in his jeans she imagined what he looked like out of them. For some reason, she felt no reservations about spending the night with a total stranger. She wanted him and could tell he wanted her.

They clumsily made their way up to her room on the second floor and he took her swipe key from her hand and opened the door. Nicolette didn't have to worry about what to say because as soon as the door was closed, he pressed her back against the wall and began to kiss her passionately. It had excited Nicolette in every way. His lips were strong but soft and his tongue was sensual and unobtrusive. He kissed her on her ears and her neck while his hands wandered about her body firm but swiftly. Nicolette instinctively pushed him back because for a moment it was too fast. After a breath, she gathered herself and pushed him back on the opposite wall in the entryway and began unbuttoning his shirt revealing his strong shoulders and muscular chest. After a close-up glimpse of the tattoo on his arm, she saw it was an image of a jarhead with the words "bad boy" below it. He guided her back on the bed, unfastened her jeans, and pulled them down past her feet. Nicolette took off her shirt. Jamie unbuttoned his jeans slowly at the foot of the bed. He watched intently while Nicolette wiggled around, unclasped her bra, and threw it to the ground.

Nicolette could see him hard in his briefs as she slowly lowered and removed her moist panties down past her feet. She held them for a moment on one finger as if taunting him, smiled and threw them at him. She missed and they both smiled. It was as if someone fired a starting pistol and he quickly dropped his own briefs only giving her a quick glimpse of him fully naked before pouncing on top of her. He kissed her lips, neck, breasts, and stomach before he wrapped an arm under each of her thighs, lifted her up, and lowered his face between her legs. After a few minutes, he made his way back up her body to look her in the eyes and plunge into her. Nicolette didn't know if it was because she was nervous or the alcohol or why the reason she couldn't come, but he did.

They didn't say a word to each other, laid next to each other exhausted on the bed, and fell asleep. He held her all night long in his strong tan bicep and she fell fast to sleep. Jamie awakened Nicolette from the best sleep she'd had in a long time and told her he was sorry but he had to go to work. He jotted his number down on a pad of paper on the nightstand and kissed her passionately goodbye.

"Please call," he said.

Nicolette didn't speak but just watched him with her sleepy eyes trying to take in how gorgeous he was. He watched her as he dressed and before he left, he ran back to give her another kiss quickly before disappearing out the door. Nicolette felt so much warmth from him. His eagerness to be near her was palpable. It sparked something in her and to her surprise, she wondered for a split second if it was love. Nicolette smiled wide as she threw herself back down on the pillow, hugged one of the extra pillows pretending it was Jamie and fell fast asleep.

Chapter Ten

When Nicolette woke, she was shocked to see the clock read just past noon. Her head was both filled with immediate thoughts of Jamie and a mild ache from the tequila the night before. She hadn't drunk like that in a long time and wasn't sure she respected herself for doing it. She also wasn't sure she would have had the guts to let go of all of her inhibitions and give herself to Jamie as freely without it.

Nicolette quickly shook away her thoughts and got into the shower. As she lathered up her body with the shower gel and hot water, she closed her eyes and imagined Jamie there with her. It was his hands caressing her warm soapy wet skin. As she massaged the shampoo into her hair her fingers were him kissing playfully on the back of her neck.

Once showered and dressed Nicolette made her way downstairs to the lobby. There was a small side room next to the front desk selling small bags of crackers, potato chips, gum, and other items travelers may want. Nicolette opted for the foil package containing two pain relievers for her headache, brought it to the counter, paid and headed out the door to the Rusty Spur for a quick bite to eat. She had a big day ahead of her to find a place to live and she was already off to a late start.

Once inside the bar and grill, Nicolette took a seat at one of the booths by the window. The same waitress from the night before was there again. It only took a moment for her to notice Nicolette and she came right over to the booth.

"Well…well, hi there. Guess that salad was so good you had to come back and see us again huh?" she chided.

"I guess you could say that. Ha-ha. Do they ever let you go home, or do you just work around the clock and have a cot in the back?" she said.

"Pretty much. We are short-handed and looking for another waitress to help out. Until they find someone, I will be working a lot of doubles. What can I get you? More cranberry juice, a salad, a hot cowboy with a bad boy tattoo?" she said.

Nicolette was embarrassed but enjoyed the waitress's sarcasm. She could feel her face turning hot and likely bright red but accepted the challenge of her banter.

"Possibly, but I can't tell you my deep dark secrets when I don't even know your first name," she said.

"Oh, I am sorry. I lost my damn nametag. I keep meaning to make a new one but I get busy and forget. My name is Maria," she said.

"Well Maria, my name is Nicolette and I will have a burger and fries, no cheese, extra pickles please, and a…"

"Cranberry Juice?" Maria interrupted.

"Ha-ha no thank you. Got any remedies for too many tequila shots?" Nicolette asked.

"I have just the thing," Maria replied.

Maria kept the menu she hadn't yet given Nicolette and went to put the order in. When she returned, she was holding what she said to be a glass of tomato juice with exactly thirteen shakes of hot sauce in it and a celery stalk. She put the glass down in front of

Nicolette and slid a piece of paper onto the table,

smiled with a wink and walked away. Nicolette

inspected the paper and saw it was a job application.

As she pondered the reason for Maria placing it there,

she took a sip of the tomato juice certain by the taste

it was not just tomato juice and hot sauce in there.

Nicolette wasn't a stranger to mixed drinks and that

innocent glass of tomato juice was obviously a

Bloody Mary. A good one too.

Nicolette smiled inside and drew a fast conclusion she

was going to like living in Willette already. In less

than twenty-four hours she met a seemingly great

guy, a waitress for a friend and possibly a job. As

Nicolette filled out the application it was pretty easy

since she had only worked one job as a hostess at the

restaurant her mother waitressed for. She was glad

she could at least write in having a GED instead of simply scribbling in dropout. Nicolette looked forward to being able to list herself as a college graduate on a future application.

Maria and Nicolette bonded over bits and pieces of their abridged life stories in between Maria having to wait on other tables. Although they had many differences, they appeared to see life very similar and their sense of humor was the same. It was obvious they were indeed going to be friends. Nicolette laid cash down on top of the check on her table. Maria cleared the table of Nicolette's plate, cup, money, the application, and they said their goodbyes.

Nicolette came out of the front door of the Rusty Spur and the sun was shining bright. The few sips of the Bloody Mary she'd had did make her feel better. The pain relievers and the food probably helped too. On her way to the car, she heard a male voice hollering her name across the parking lot. It was Jamie. Her heart leaped into her throat and as she turned toward him, he made his way across the lot. Nicolette wasn't sure what the etiquette was supposed to be after you sleep with a guy the first night you meet him. She was certain she looked awkward figuring out what to do with herself when he came into her personal space.

He scooped her up and twirled her around hugging her waist, set her down and planted a soft, passionate kiss on her mouth. Nicolette's own passion turned to self-consciousness when she remembered the onions she had on her burger. As she prayed in her head that she didn't taste gross for Jaime he interrupted her thoughts and removed all doubt.

"Mm...mm onions. I love onions," he said.

She lightly swatted his arm and laughed. Jaime laughed too and asked her where she was off to and sarcastically asked her why she hadn't called him yet. The way they both enjoyed playful banter felt so natural.

"You only left my room nine hours ago duh," she said.

"Ha-ha, I know," he said.

"How do you survive on two hours of sleep and work all day? I slept until noon and I was still hurting," she said.

"I am the perfect species. It is all the beer I drink. I don't need sleep," he said.

Nicolette rolled her eyes and laughed. Jamie had such a sarcastic nature. Like Maria, he could keep up with Nicolette's banter. Sometimes Nicolette remained quiet in situations because people didn't understand her lightning-fast wit. When she encountered someone with the same skill it became a playful spar trying to one-up each other like a sport. They exchanged a few more sarcastic quips with each other and inquired about their individual plans for the day. Jamie asked Nicolette if she wanted to postpone her to-do list and go over to his place instead. Without a second of pause, she quickly agreed.

Jamie led the way to his car and Nicolette followed closely behind. He was careful to make certain if he went through the stoplight, she would have enough time to get through it too or he would stop on the yellow so he didn't lose her. Nicolette felt so energized being with Jamie. It seemed she had the same effect on him unless he was just always like that. How would she have known? They pulled into a large parking lot where several buildings with three-story connected townhouses in clusters towered above. A large pool sat in the middle of those. Jamie's unit was one of the ones facing the pool.

They made their way through a wooden gate about waste high and onto a small patio that led to his front door. There were two run-down plastic patio chairs and a dead plant in a pot. Nicolette was curious about the dirty pair of roller skates tipped over in the tiny grass patch alongside the patio and the hula hoop leaning against what looked like the door to an exterior storage closet. She didn't say anything as he led her into the front door and closed it behind them.

The bottom floor was fairly large and carpeted from one side to the other and laid out like a great room with a dinette and chandelier to the left and living room with a large cabinet tv against the wall to the right. His furniture was mismatched. Half of a red leather sectional couch and a separate brown fabric loveseat shoved up against the side of it where the missing sectional pieces should have been. Jaime went into the kitchenette off of the dining area separated only by a tall serving counter. Nicolette nervously took a spot on the front edge of one of the red sectional seats and leaned her elbow onto the arm. Jaime came around the corner with a big smile on his face with two bottled beers and handed her one and started up the stairs.

"Come on. I will give you a tour," he said.

Nicolette could see there was a storage closet door under the stairs and a bathroom to the side of it as she trailed closely behind him. The stairs made a sharp turn halfway up and then went up again. There were two closed doors she assumed were bedrooms and an open one which was clearly a bathroom. There was another set of stairs going even further up.

"Where do those steps lead?" she asked.

"There is a loft up there," he said.

Jaime opened the closed door closest to the bathroom to reveal the master bedroom. There was a large four-poster bed up against a wall with a huge window, a desk, a ceiling fan, and a walk-in closet. It was fairly tidy like the downstairs, but dusty and definitely looked like a bachelor lived there. There was another door leading to the same bathroom connected to the hallway. Nicolette thought the set up was unique. Jamie set his beer down on the desk, grabbed Nicolette's from her hand and set it down next to his. He placed his hands on both of her hips and pulled her strongly towards him. He laid back on the bed guiding her up on top of him as he kissed her and groped her. Within minutes they were completely naked and enjoying each other's bodies just like the night before but this time sober and not as rushed. Unlike the night before, Nicolette came twice before Jaime did. She couldn't believe sex could be like that. Her feelings were already so strong for Jamie as if she had known him forever even though she didn't really know him at all. Nicolette laid next to Jaime tucked under his arm wrapped around her with her head on his chest. His skin was so smooth and his muscles firm. The smell of his cologne was enticing although she didn't know what kind it was. His heartbeat strong and sure in his chest. The sound comforted her.

"I need some food," he said.

"I had a burger at the Spur," she said.

"Oh yes, the onions. Well, you can watch me eat," he said.

Nicolette swatted him lightly on the chest and they both rose from the bed, pulled their clothes on and she followed him back downstairs. Jamie headed directly for the kitchen and Nicolette let him know she would be right there as she stopped to go into the bathroom next to the staircase. As she pushed the door all the way open, she was startled by what she saw. She entered the room, closed the door and her eyes scanned as she sat down on the toilet next to the sink. There was a stackable washer and dryer with a mountain of unwashed clothes next to it on the floor. There were childlike watercolor art scenes and handprints from finger paints taped randomly on the walls. Nicolette looked down at the pile of clothing and was able to detect the majority of it was for a child. It looked like girls' clothing. Nicolette stood to her feet, nervously pulled her jeans up, flushed the toilet, and stared at herself wide-eyed in the mirror as she washed her hands.

Nicolette paused before opening the door to join Jamie in the kitchen. The scenarios created by what she had seen started swirling in her head. When she reached the kitchen, she stood in the dining area leaned upon the tall serving counter and watched Jamie make a sandwich on the small counter next to the sink. Jamie heard her there, turned to her and smiled.

"Are you sure you don't want one?" he asked.

"I am sure," she said.

He wrapped his sandwich in a napkin and grabbed two more beers from the fridge. He walked over to the front door and stood there signaling for Nicolette to open it for him. She opened the door and followed him out where they each took a seat in a patio chair. Nicolette took the beers from Jamie and set them on the ground between their chairs. She sat awkwardly and didn't speak as he ate his sandwich like a stray dog with a plate of raw meat. As her eyes scanned the patio again her stomach twisted inside as she stared at the roller skates.

"Are you okay?" Jamie asked.

"Oh. Yeah. Sure. Can I ask you something?" she said.

"Of course," he said.

"Do you have children?" she asked.

Jamie's face stiffened as his smile dissipated. He appeared nervous and sat up taller and cleared his throat.

"Yes, I have a daughter," he said.

Nicolette's heart sank in her stomach. She reviewed everything she could remember from their conversation the night before. They had talked for hours and even though the tequila was flowing she was certain she would have remembered him tell her something like that.

"I don't remember that coming up in conversation last night. That is kind of a big thing," she said.

"Look Nicolette it's no big deal. I just didn't want to scare you away," he said.

"Where is she now? What is her name? Where is her mother? I am assuming there is a mother," she said.

"She is with her mother today or probably at daycare. Her name is Tallulah. I call her Lulu. Her mother's name is Keres. We aren't together anymore," he said.

Nicolette's anxiety calmed a little. Jamie convinced her to bring her beer back inside the house so he could tell her everything. They each took a spot on the couch and began talking. Jamie explained his tumultuous marriage to Keres and how he stayed as long as he did because he loved his daughter. Keres eventually cheated on him with a man she was working with and she left Jamie for him. Nicolette wondered how he married such a callous woman who would steal half of his furniture and hold it hostage unless he bought it back from her. It was the reason his living room was furnished the way it was. His ease of sharing his pain and candor about the meaningless relationships he'd had since the demise of his marriage drew Nicolette closer to him. He bared his soul to her and even cried a little. No man had ever opened up to her the way he did. The hours slipped away and it was night time again.

Nicolette told Jamie she should get back to her motel room and get some sleep so she could get up early and go find a place to live. She forwent a whole day of apartment searching but it didn't feel wasted at all. She stood up a little tipsy from all of the beers they had consumed while they were talking and Jamie didn't think she should drive.

"Why don't you stay with me," he said.

"But I don't have my toothbrush or any clothes to change into. I really need to find an apartment tomorrow," she said.

"No. I mean why don't you move in here. I have plenty of room. Lulu is only here a few days a week. She will love you. You don't have to pay rent or anything. Just see how it goes. If it works out it will be cheaper for you once you are enrolled in school too" he said.

Nicolette was shocked. Everything was moving so fast with Jamie. Everything about everything had moved so fast since she came to Willette. The thought living in an apartment by herself did seem kind of lonely but she just met this guy. Maybe it was all too good to be true. She thought for a moment about all of the things in her life that never looked too good for anything and they were true. If she turned him down, she might regret it. It crossed her mind that at least something too good to be true for a short time might be better than dependable misery.

"I can't believe I am saying this but yes," she said.

"Hell yes. I promise this will work. Let's go get your stuff. I will drive," he said.

Jamie grabbed Nicolette and kissed her slowly. Time stood still for a moment. They let go of each other, Nicolette grabbed her purse and Jamie his car keys.

They left the townhouse to go get Nicolette's things from her room and check her out of the motel. They held hands across the console of Jamie's car as he drove. Nicolette couldn't help but dream of the future.

Chapter Eleven

Jamie had already left for work when Nicolette got

out of bed that day. She loved the way the light from

the huge window over the bed warmed the whole

room in the morning. It bounced off of the high

vaulted ceiling and into the loft upstairs. Nicolette

wondered what was up there. She stepped down from

the bed and even though she was alone she tiptoed up

the stairs to the loft and peeked around the corner.

First, she saw a beanbag chair and a table with a lamp

on top. The entire floor was covered in toys both

broken and whole, crumpled paper, a few pillows and

blankets, and countless other random items. All

clearly belonging to a child. It looked like the room

had been ransacked and picked through like a flea

market or neighborhood garage sale. Each abandoned

item told its own story. Nicolette had a lot in common with those toys.

Nicolette noticed a small door in the wall. It was too small for an adult to go into or even a child unless on their knees. When she opened the door, she saw a play kitchen set and random items thrown about the floor just like in the main loft. On her hands and knees, she crawled in just far enough to reach the chain pull which turned on the light. There were crayon drawings of nothing in particular all over the walls broken up by half-peeled stickers and smudges. She tugged on the chain once more to turn out the light, backed out of the door and stood up with her hands on her hips looking around. Everything up there felt chaotic and sad. Nicolette started to get a vision of what might have taken place there. She didn't like what she saw.

After she had seen enough, she headed back down the stairs and stopped on the middle landing. She paused outside the unopened door next to the master bedroom for a moment wondering if she really wanted to go in there. Nicolette opened the door. There were cartoon curtains hanging half torn off of a wooden rod over the window, a broken lamp on the floor and bunkbeds unmade missing parts of their bedding. There were shoes and clothing on the floor and wrappers from snacks. The closet doors were off of their spindles and the closet also looked ransacked with broken and empty hangers but still a lot of clothing left behind. Nicolette rested her gaze on an oversized and overstuffed gorilla wearing a yellow shirt and holding a banana. His eyes were wild and crazy looking. She thought that gorilla and his eyes must have suited the situation in that room perfectly.

Nicolette decided to do some cleaning and organizing in the townhouse. She wanted it to feel less chaotic when Jamie got home. If she was going to meet this young Lulu at some point, she wanted her to have a calm and organized place to come to. Something Nicolette didn't have when she was young. She also had to run-up to the Rusty Spur and update her application with a phone number now that she had one. She showered, got dressed, and went downstairs to start a load of the laundry from the bathroom floor. Nicolette grabbed a piece of paper and a pen she found in a kitchen drawer and inspected the phone for what the number might have been. The phone rang loudly in her face and she jumped back, fear quickly turning into laughter. The caller ID said, Keres Tanner. Nicolette realized she had moved in with a man after knowing him for barely a day and didn't even know his last name until that moment. She backed away from the phone unsure if she should answer it. She remembered Jamie had already given her his phone number at the motel that first night, found it in her purse, and headed out the door for the Rusty Spur.

Nicolette had a hard time finding her way back to the bar. She was so intent on not losing sight of Jamie's car on the way to his townhouse she didn't really log in all the street signs and turns. Luckily, she found her way there after passing a taco stand, she recognized and a billboard for a guy claiming his pillow would be the most comfortable pillow Nicolette would ever own.

When Nicolette entered the bar, it was busier than she thought it would be. The lunch rush was apparently different when they first opened at eleven on this day than it was after Noon the day before. They did have a hostess seating people though. Nicolette decided to sit at the bar to avoid all of the confusion like she did at the diner while she was on the road. They had already served her alcohol twice so she figured they wouldn't care if she sat there now. She stood up straight, put her chin up and acted like she wasn't nervous.

The only seat open at the bar was right in the middle between two tan muscle-bound men eating lunch. Their soiled tattered clothes and work boots told her they were probably construction workers. Most of the bar was full of them. The bar surface was unclean with dirty glasses and some crumbs left-over from whoever sat there last. The stools were so close to each other Nicolette felt her jeans pockets rub against one of the men's legs as she hopped up to take her seat. He turned to her and smiled.

"Damn you can rub that ass on me anytime girl," he said.

"Ha-ha, no thank you, I have a hot cowboy at home for that stuff," she said.

The bar erupted with laughter towards the outspoken man. His buddies sitting closest to him repeated what she had said to the seat next to them like the telephone game. As it spread around the entire bar each of them looked at her with a grin of approval and respect for putting him in his place. The man was a little embarrassed but he also seemed to have respect for Nicolette's quick wit. He outstretched his arm to shake her hand. Nicolette took his hand softly, grinned and nodded her head.

"Hi, little lady. My name is Garth. Nice to meet you," he said.

"My name is Nicolette. Nice to meet you too Garth," she said.

The rest of his buddies introduced themselves as well and soon they were bantering with each other like a bunch of friends around the lunch table at school. Tom the bartender filled her a tall coke with ice and Maria brought her a club sandwich and her application to update before running off to take care of her tables for the rest of the lunch rush. By the time Nicolette had finished half of her sandwich, the bar had mostly cleared out. There were still a few tables Maria tended to but her new construction worker friends had gone back to work. There were only two people left sitting on barstools other than her.

Once Maria and the other server on duty had collected their tips, helped the busboy clean up the dining area, and wiped down the bar top she returned to where Nicolette was sitting. She brought a box for the rest of Nicolette's sandwich and retrieved the application. Maria glanced down to see Nicolette's phone number and her head sprang back up. She stared wide-eyed at Nicolette and her jaw dropped open. Her mouth returned to a sheepish grin but she was still wide-eyed.

"Hey, that is my brother's phone number. I know you two got along great the other night but wow!" she said.

Nicolette looked like a deer in front of headlights. She froze and could feel herself light up bright red. All of a sudden Nicolette matched some of Maria's facial features to Jamie's in her mind. They looked different enough and it never occurred to her they were related. But their personalities were very similar at it started to make perfect sense.

"Oh my God. I didn't know he was your brother. Is that okay?" she said.

"Damn, of course, it is okay! You are way better than that bitch he married. He deserves someone kind and fun like you in his life for once," she said.

Nicolette breathed a sigh of relieve and the heat on her face turned down several notches. She really liked Jamie. She also really liked Maria and didn't want to cause any problems, create any drama or worse have to choose between them. Nicolette had enough drama to last the rest of her life at that point and she usually ran from the first sign of trouble like a scared cat. After hearing how Maria felt about Keres, Nicolette was extremely glad she chose not to answer the phone earlier before she left the townhouse.

Nicolette noticed a short husky man with a scruffy grey mustache and glasses entering the bar area behind Maria. He looked very serious as he approached them. He wore a wrinkly white long-sleeve dress shirt and a pale blue tie hanging too short on his portly belly. It was almost impossible to see the belt holding up his cheap khaki dress pants. The tie matched his eyes that started to twinkle as he rested his elbows on the bar next to Maria and stared across it at Nicolette. At first, Nicolette thought he was going to ask her for ID and make her leave the bar top. Thankfully she was only drinking a soda that day. Instead, he smiled wide at her and went to shake her hand. Nicolette smiled back and offered him her hand in return.

"Hi, Nicolette. I'm Mack. I am the manager here at this fine establishment. I hear you are looking to fill the spot we have open for a waitress. Is that correct?" he said.

"Oh. Absolutely sir. I would love to if you will have me," she said.

"Well you come highly recommended by Maria here and if she likes you than I do too. This place wouldn't survive without Maria so congratulations. It is yours," he said.

Nicolette felt warm towards Maria for recommending her with how little they actually knew each other. It seemed since Nicolette prayed with Mitchell that day things started randomly happening for her like that. She looked at Maria with a mixture of expressions both surprised and thankful. She offered her hand back to Mack filled with gratitude.

As Nicolette processed the idea that she just got hired without not so much as a formal interview she felt on top of the world. Only knocked a bit down from the top when Mack spoke as he walked away from the bar.

"Just one thing. No more tequila shots or Bloody Mary's in my bar until you are twenty-one. I read your application and I am good at math. You can start tomorrow. Maria can help you with the rest," he said.

Nicolette turned red again and positioned her shocked expression back towards Maria. She responded to Mack with her best military impression.

"Yes sir!" she said.

Maria and Nicolette held hands across the bar and giggled like two school girls.

"Oh my God Maria! Thank you!" she said.

"No problem Nicolette and don't worry about that old grump, he is a big softy. Not just his belly!" she said.

They both erupted in laughter. Maria told Nicolette what time to be there the next day, some tips on how to wear her hair and what kind of clothes to wear. She grabbed her a half apron all of the front of the house employees wore with an embroidered logo for the Rust Spur on it. They fumbled around with a label gun and made Nicolette a nametag before Maria had to get to a couple of tables that had just been seated in her station. Nicolette wanted to get back to the townhouse and finish cleaning up before Jamie got home from work anyway.

Nicolette drove away from the Rusty Spur with a new sense of pride. As she took inventory of all of the great things that had happened to her so quickly since she moved to Willette the thought occurred to her she should probably call her mother to let her know she was all right. Nicolette made her way back to the townhouse with ease as if she had been going there for years instead of just a couple of days. As she entered the house, she noticed the caller ID box next to the phone was blinking blue signaling new calls. She figured it was probably just the one phone call from Keres before she left but when she looked at the box it showed the maximum amount of calls that could be logged on the device. Twenty-five. That sparked Nicolette's curiosity as she pressed the button to flip through the names on the box. She realized they were all from Keres Tanner.

As Nicolette finished tidying up bedrooms, cleaning floors and disinfected the kitchen and bathrooms questions swirled in her head of why Keres called so many times. The only spaces Nicolette avoided were the loft and the playroom attached to it. While she was upstairs putting the closet doors back on and repairing the lamp in Lulu's bedroom the phone had rung at least five more times but she didn't answer it. Part of her felt too new to the scenario to feel like it was her place to answer it especially to talk to Keres. She knew it couldn't have been anyone calling for her after all only three people even knew she lived there yet and she had just left two of them.

The ringing phone did remind her to call her mother though. It was a very brief call just to update Valerie on the trip, give her the address and phone number, and to let her know Nicolette was safe. Just as Nicolette hung up with her mother Jamie came home through the front door looking tired from work. As soon as she saw him, she ran to him, jumped up on him wrapping her legs around his waist and her arms around his neck. Luckily, she was petite and thin and although he wobbled a bit, he was strong enough to withstand her attack. He dropped his lunchbox to the sofa and wrapped his arms around her too. Their lips locked for a good few minutes before he put her down to find the floor with her feet.

As Jamie retrieved two beers from the refrigerator he glanced around his clean kitchen, dining area and living room marveling at all of Nicolette's hard work. When he threw his t-shirt into the dirty laundry, he could actually see the hamper in the bathroom now that Nicolette had washed all of the dirty clothes once piled there.

"Damn Nicolette, thank you for doing all of this! It looks amazing! So nice to have a woman's touch around here again," he said.

Nicolette beamed as she sat on the couch sipped her beer and watched Jamie ascend the stairs to get a clean shirt. She eagerly waited for his reaction when he saw upstairs. As Jamie wandered around up there while putting on his shirt, he hollered down to her.

"Lulu's room looks great! Damn you are hot, you can clean and fix things! What a catch!" he said.

As Nicolette leaned on the back of the couch congratulating herself for evoking the exact response from Jamie, she was hoping for she heard him holler one more time as he came down the stairwell to join her on the couch.

"I guess you didn't have time to do the loft huh?" he asked.

"Oh, no I didn't, sorry," she said.

Nicolette's joy turned to immediate shame and disappointment in herself. She shouldn't have spent so much time at the Rusty Spur then she would have had time to organize the loft. His comment reminded her of how her mother would criticize the one thing she missed while trying to do something nice for her. Although taken back by his words she assumed he didn't mean it the way it sounded and let it go.

"We are almost out of beer. I am going to run up and grab some more and something to make for dinner. Lulu will be here at six o'clock and there is no food in the house. She likes her juice boxes and Cheetos," he said.

"Oh okay, you had better hurry. It is already four-thirty. Do you want some company?" she said.

He kissed her on the forehead and headed swiftly towards the front door.

"No. That is okay. You have done more than enough today. Put your feet up and enjoy your beer. I got this," he said.

Nicolette rose to her feet and watched out the window as Jamie closed the door. He was so handsome and she tingled at how good he looked in his jeans and tight t-shirt. Before he left the patio, he leaned down and adjusted the trash can that sat on the patio. His body was blocking her view of the can so she wasn't sure exactly what he was doing. After he was out of sight around the corner Nicolette creeped out onto the patio and looked at the can. Maybe she had dropped some trash on the patio or something during her cleaning, but Jamie never opened the lid so it made her curious. Looking down at the ground Nicolette could see what looked like a wad of cash sticking out underneath the bottom of it. She wasn't sure why Jamie put it there. It wasn't there earlier in the day.

Nicolette tossed her empty beer bottle into the trash can and left the cash there. Thoughts of how nervous she was to meet Lulu pushed the curiosity about the money quickly from her mind. She went back in and opened one of the last beers and went upstairs to freshen herself up for the big introduction soon to take place. As she brushed her hair, pulled it up in a fresh ponytail, and reapplied some makeup in the bathroom mirror she heard the front door open downstairs. A loud brash female voice hollered Jamie's name. Nicolette had a habit of locking doors when she was home alone from too much experience of what can happen when you don't while she was growing up. She knew she had locked the front door to the townhouse when she came back inside. Nicolette heard little footsteps clomping quickly up the stairs too fast to be an adult.

Disoriented by what was happening Nicolette cautiously stepped out of the upstairs bathroom and turned to go downstairs to see who had just let themselves into their home, obviously with a key. Nicolette was startled when a small girl no older than four ran into her legs at the top of the stairs. Nicolette had to catch the little girl from falling back down the stairs after bouncing off of her. The girl had unkept long brown hair and remnants of something dark and sticky on her cheeks and around her mouth. She was dressed in a pink frilly shirt with stains on the front, jean pants that looked too small on her with high water pant legs and no shoes. Her feet were filthy all around. Nicolette tried to smile at the little girl through her shock of how disheveled she looked.

"You must be Lulu," Nicolette said.

"Yep," she said.

Lulu didn't seem curious about Nicolette at all and didn't seem to miss a beat after their collision. She pushed right past her and made her way quickly and loudly up to the loft. Nicolette froze on the middle landing wondering if she should follow her up there and try to engage with Lulu more. She was more interested in that idea than she was in going down to greet the loud intrusive woman downstairs who let herself into the townhouse without so much as a knock or a ring of the doorbell. Nicolette figured it would be rude if she didn't so she went down to greet Keres in the living room. As she slowly and timidly descended the staircase she heard Jamie's voice speak to Keres as he entered the house.

Nicolette hurried her steps and when she got to the bottom, she saw Jamie standing by the open door and Keres with her hands on her hips barking orders at Jamie in an angry rude voice. Keres's back was to Nicolette and when Jamie looked past his ex-wife and spoke lovingly to Nicolette, she turned around to see who he was talking to.

"Who the hell are you?" Keres asked.

Nicolette froze near the bottom of the stairs now reluctant to approach the woman and shot Jamie a look like a plea to rescue her from ire from the tyrant in between them. Jamie quickly came to Nicolette's rescue, pushed past Keres and escorted Nicolette to a seat at the dining room table and turned back to finish dealing with the issue before him.

"Wow you really traded up to a real hardbody, didn't you? Is she living here?" Keres said.

"Her name is Nicolette. Yes, she lives here and yes I definitely traded up" he said.

Nicolette sat still and awkward staring out the window at the patio studying the open gate, the trash can, and the door on the storage closet outside. She kept her eyes darting from all of those things to avoid eye contact with the angry woman in the room who seemed to despise her very existence. She peeked glances over at Jamie as Keres stormed upstairs and came back down with an armload of what looked like Lulu's clothes Nicolette had washed and put away earlier that day. As Keres neared the still open door, she looked back at Jamie with so much disdain.

"I will be back to get Lulu at eleven o'clock. As long as that bitch is here, she is not sleeping over," she said.

Keres turned to Nicolette who was still seated at the table. The fire and hatred in her eyes felt like it burned through Nicolette, right through her skull.

"He is great at first but wait until you have spent five years being ignored when he never listens to you," she said.

Nicolette stayed silent with a look of shock on her face. Jamie said nothing he just put the beer and groceries away as if nothing was happening. Keres slammed the front door behind her. Nicolette watched out the window intently as Keres nudged the trash can with her foot and leaned down to get the cash Jamie had put underneath it. She dropped a few pieces of the clean clothes she was carrying onto the ground. Keres made two attempts to bend down and pick them up but she dropped another piece each time she did. Keres gave up, kicked the trash can over, and stormed off leaving a couple of items behind on the ground as she went. She attempted to slam the gate but it bounced back open from the force. Jamie exhaled forcefully with a sigh of relief, grabbed a beer, and sat down on the couch silent staring up at the ceiling. Nicolette sat still on her chair like it was an anchor holding her to the floor preventing her from floating away as she wondered what in the hell, she had gotten herself into this time.

Chapter Twelve

During the next couple of years, Nicolette fell into a comfortable routine with Jamie and Lulu. The passion between her and Jamie stayed on high for a long time. So did the tumultuous triangle between them and Keres. Nicolette convinced Jamie to get back the house key from Keres so she could feel safe knowing she wouldn't wake up to anymore surprise visitors in the house who hated her. Jamie still put cash under the trash can for Keres for quite a while. Nicolette never told him she knew. Keres still called obsessively but Lulu had become an inconvenience to her busy dating life so she spent weeks at a time in Jamie's custody most months.

Nicolette had learned the parenting routine of discipline and nurturing. She got good at packing lunches and juggling her job with the drop off and pickups to and from school when Lulu was home. It was tough but Nicolette finished her Associates' Degree at the Community College. She managed to keep it all together and get it done with honors in English. Nicolette and Lulu were very close. Keres hated it and constantly tried to sabotage their bond. Nicolette dealt with it the best she could but eventually, the division worked and Lulu's loyalty was forced to her mother's benefit.

When Keres demanded full custody, Jamie didn't argue but it came out to Nicolette that prior to that time Jamie and Keres had never been officially divorced. Once they were, the money under the trash can routine stopped. Many things Nicolette didn't understand became clearer then but felt she was already in love with Jamie, committed to him, and couldn't imagine her life without him. As bad as it was sometimes it still wasn't as bad as it used to be before she came to Willette.

The trust between Nicolette and Jamie started to deteriorate as she caught him in small lies. He was obviously good at omitting important information but the small lies made her wonder what big lies he may have been telling. Jamie often worked extra shifts and sometimes didn't come home until late at night. Sometimes not at all. Nicolette had an Associate's Degree and hopes and aspirations of going to University and getting her bachelor's degree. She worked her shifts at the Rusty Spur and spent a lot of time with Maria shopping and partying. They were a dynamic duo at work and in their off time. Tom the bartender looked out for both of them. The three of them were the best of friends.

One day Nicolette and Maria were both working a lunch shift. Tom was bartending and no hostess was on duty. Mack was helping to seat people while Nicolette and Maria split the restaurant but they also had to seat people too. Maria placed someone at one of Nicolette's booths and approached Nicolette while she entered an order at the computer beside the bar.

"Hey Nicolette, see that guy at fourteen? He asked for your section. He is kind of cute. Who is he?" she said.

"I don't know I can't see him good from here. I will be there in a minute," she said.

Maria whisked off to take care of her tables. Nicolette had the same graceful serving style as Maria did. A manager from a Denny's down the road had been in for lunch one day. It was standard practice for him to visit other eating establishments to recruit waitresses with skills he liked to come work for him for more pay. He told Nicolette she looked like a dancer while she worked. She remembered thinking the same thing about Shelby until her catty behavior over Paul. Nicolette was flattered and enticed by the higher pay. Mack couldn't match what she was offered so she accepted it and worked at Denny's for a few weeks. The other waitresses there hated Nicolette. They called her the manager's whore pet. Nicolette was far from a whore and she resented it but put up with it until the manager cornered her in the dish room, tried to kiss her, and groped her breasts. Nicolette went crawling back to Mack who was just happy to see her and eagerly welcomed her home to the Rusty Spur.

Nicolette made her way to table fourteen and as she approached, she couldn't believe who it was, Kyle. He was studying the menu and drinking water Maria had brought him while he waited. She was nervous to approach him. So many memories flooded back. She took a deep breath and said hello. Kyle raised his eyes to hers. The way he looked at her hadn't changed after all those years. He wasn't as handsome as she remembered. He appeared ragged and worn. Maybe he always looked that way and Nicolette couldn't see it then because she was ragged and worn too.

"Hi, Nicolette. Wow, you are still gorgeous," he said.

Nicolette didn't know what to say so she thanked him in an awkward pleasant bank teller sort of way. She didn't want to give him any hope of rekindling what they shared but for some reason, she knew that was exactly why he was there. As they made small talk and she took the order things he said made her feel uneasy. People tend to suck her back into their flight pattern because of her high capacity for empathy and desire to be kind. She didn't want it to happen this time. Nicolette finished jotting down his food and drink and cornered Maria at the back of the bar.

"You have to take this table. I will take any of yours off your hands but I can't wait on him," she said.

"Why? What the heck? So, you do know him. Of course, I will take it for you no problem," she said.

Maria snatched the order page from Nicolette's fingers, smiled, and walked tall to the terminal to place the order. Nicolette knew Maria would have her back. Maria was a loyal and trustworthy friend. Nicolette managed to avoid Kyle's table as she tended to all of her other customers. He watched her intently as she worked. He looked as confused as a lost puppy. Nicolette still managed to avoid him until he paid his tab and left. Nicolette spilled the whole story to Maria at the bar after their shift while they ate their comp meal together and had a few Bloody Mary's. That was their drink of choice when they spent time with one another. Sometimes on wine nights, they would sit on the townhouse patio while Jamie was at work and kill three or four bottles spouting girl talk.

Nicolette cut the Bloody Mary's short this time because she was still a bit shaken from seeing Kyle again. She said goodbye to Maria and returned home. As her key turned in the lock, she heard the phone ring. Nicolette hurried into the door shoving it closed behind her and got to the phone before it stopped. The caller ID said unavailable.

"Hello?" she said.

"Hi Nicolette," he said.

Her mind raced to attach an identity to the male voice on the other end of the phone. She realized it was Kyle. Her heart jumped into her throat and she stood silent with the phone hanging off of her ear. Kyle gave her such a strange vibe at the bar she was almost fearful of him.

"Why did you avoid me at the bar, Nicolette? I traveled all of this way here to see you and you just ignore me? Can you meet me for a drink? Come on it isn't like I am going to beat you up or anything," he said.

Nicolette had a flash vision crash into her consciousness. She pictured herself meeting Kyle at a park. They shared a few beers and he got angry with her. There was a struggle. He raised his open hand to her and hit her across the face. He threw himself on her and raped her in the grass near a merry-go-round.

"Don't call me anymore!" she said.

Nicolette didn't wait for a response and slammed the phone down on the cradle. She wanted to unplug it so it couldn't ring again but wouldn't risk missing a call from Jamie or not being available for Lulu. Shaking she looked at the front door remembering she hadn't locked it. She ran over to the door and quickly locked both locks and closed the blinds on the windows. Nicolette sat down and had a few beers on the couch watching tv waiting for Jamie to come home. A loud commercial woke her up about eleven o'clock and Jamie still wasn't there so she went upstairs, got ready for bed and tucked herself in. For the first time in a long time, she cried herself to sleep.

Nicolette was awakened by Jamie fumbling to take his boots off in the walk-in closet. When he found the switch for the light, he turned it on and it hurt Nicolette's eyes. She asked him where he had been and why he hadn't called. He was visibly drunk and falling all over the place. Jamie got defensive and called her the usual names he called her when he was avoiding telling her something. He developed a strategy to accuse Nicolette of absurd things and call her names until she cowered and retreated into silence or tears. When he slid into bed and turned his back towards her, she was certain his cologne smelled a little more like perfume than it used to. Nicolette turned her back towards him in response and cried herself to sleep for the second time that night.

When Nicolette's alarm went off the next morning Jaime was already gone. At least he left her some brewed coffee in the coffee pot. She needed it after the night before. Nicolette glided into her normal routine before work and clocked in at the Rusty Spur hoping Kyle had left town and she wouldn't have to see him again.

She worked her day shift. One of the night waitresses had called in sick for her shift and Mack asked Nicolette to stay. Maria couldn't do it because she had a date so Nicolette agreed to take it. She did have an hour break in between so she could grab something to eat and get some fresh air outside though. Nicolette's stress level had been so high for so long she almost picked up smoking again. If it wasn't for the horrible taste and smell she probably would have. It often felt as though she was reaching her breaking point. If just one more thing piled on her she was going to lose her mind. She felt herself losing her optimism for the future and falling into a familiar nihilistic pattern from her past. Nicolette's break was over and she went back inside the bar to start her next shift. It was going to be a long night.

It was easy for Nicolette to flip a switch and be the fun, outgoing, bubbly, and attentive server. People came in just to see her and sit in her station. It was an extremely busy night that night even for Nicolette. She had a hard time keeping up but she never lost her jovial, sarcastic, sparring nature people expected from her. All of her tables seemed to react positively towards her banter and have a good time. The tips were amazing.

Across the room, she could see the hostess seating her another table off in the corner of her station. She juggled drinks and plates of food dropping them off along the way to greet her new customer. As she made her way there, she poked fun at her patrons and cracked jokes they laughed hysterically at. They would throw some zingers back at her and she would burst into laughter herself. As she approached her new table, she could tell it was a man even though his back was towards her. Thankfully she could tell it was not Kyle. His hair was dark, somewhat curly, tousled about, and reached slightly down the back of his neck. Nicolette could see the collar of his shirt and shoulders as she got closer. For some reason she felt like she was moving in slow motion, having so much time to analyze his look. As she reached the side of his table and asked him if she could take his order. He peered up at her over his glasses and flashed her a wide inviting smile parting his manicured full beard and mustache. Nicolette almost fainted when she recognized who it was. It was Justin Bend.

"Yer funny," he said.

Nicolette tried to smile confidently but her lips were quivering and she was certain Justin noticed but he didn't call her on it. He was so handsome it made Nicolette weak in the knees. She shifted from foot to foot trying to keep herself standing as she stumbled through her words trying to string together a coherent sentence to find out what he wanted to order. Justin began to tell her his order and Nicolette didn't hear a word he said. The way his soft, full lips moved when he spoke made her heart race and she envisioned what they felt like pressed against hers or tasting her body. The tone of his voice was gentle and kind but confident. Justin realized Nicolette wasn't hearing him so he trailed away from listing his food order into some absurd ramblings about a bong and some Cocoa Krispies. It snapped Nicolette back into the moment.

"Oh, I am so sorry Justin! I mean I uhm think I drifted somewhere for a second. Can you repeat your order?" she said.

"So, you do know my name Nicolette," he said.

"Ha-ha, yes I guess I do but how did you know…" she started.

Justin didn't answer her but his face looked amused as he tapped her nametag on her chest with his index finger. Even his hands excited her. They were strong and his fingers long. They both laughed together and it was a relief. She was extremely embarrassed at that point but she didn't care anymore. After Justin graciously repeated his order of a veggie flatbread pizza and a draft beer Nicolette bounced away from his table filled from head to toe with both disbelief and sheer excitement. She knew this day would come somehow and it was real. Now that her vision came to fruition, she couldn't help but feel terrified. Despite her best intentions nothing ever really went the way Nicolette wanted it to in her life. Feeling both cautious and optimistic she wondered if this meeting which was years in the making was her coming face to face with her destiny or a path to the worst heartache and disappointment she had ever felt. Or knowing her luck it could be a mixture of both.

Nicolette finished waiting on the last of her other tables but Justin was still there. He was quietly reading a book and sipping on his second Scotch neat. Nicolette tried not to intrude. As she wiped down table tops, refilled salt and pepper shakers, and married ketchup bottles her eyes were magnetically drawn to Justin. His mannerisms were so casual and fluid. A couple of times she caught him as he pressed his glass to his lips and searched the room for her.

Once their eyes met their locked gaze lingered for a moment and he flashed his charismatic smile to break the tension. Nicolette had never been so sexually attracted to another man. Her whole body ached for him with just a word or a look. The way he looked at her she knew he wanted her too. When Nicolette was done cleaning up and the last call had been called, she approached Justin's table. He put down his book and pushed his glasses up his nose with his finger. Nicolette swooned over his quirky gesture.

"I am sorry you can't sleep here," she quipped.

"Oh really? Where can I sleep?" he said.

"Anywhere else but here I suppose," she said.

"I have the next four days off. If you are interested, I have a hotel room and some time," he said.

Nicolette panicked. Was this really happening? Did he finally show up just like in her vision to sweep her off her feet and whisk her away to spend the rest of her life in passion and true love? Nicolette wanted more than anything to say yes. It isn't as if Jamie should care. They were essentially strangers living in the same house at that point but she had never broken commitments or promises before no matter how badly she was treated.

"Oh, I can't do that. We can be friends if you want but I just can't do the romantic stuff right now" she said.

"I totally understand. No worries," he said.

Nicolette's head was reeling and her heart sunk into her stomach. She wanted to take back her answer and let him whisk her out the door but she didn't. It was hard for her to believe she'd had a premonition about a man she would meet years later who she never sought out show up and then say no to him. Justin looked disappointed but he was so non-judgmental towards her for turning him down. He finished his last sip of scotch and put his hand on her shoulder tenderly, said goodbye, and headed out of the bar. Nicolette wanted to scream as loud on the outside as she was on the inside as she watched him walk away. When she cleared the scotch glass from his table, she brought it to her lips and ran her tongue along the edge of the glass where his lips had been. When she picked up the napkin that was under his glass, she saw something scribbled on it. It read Justin with a phone number below.

Nicolette set the glass back down on the table and shoved the napkin into her apron, grabbed her purse from behind the bar and clocked out. She ran out the front door of the bar and scanned the parking lot for Justin. He was sitting on a bench just outside the door waiting for a taxi. He looked up when she came barreling out the door and laughed.

"Looking for someone?" he asked.

"Not anymore. I think I found him. Can I give you a lift to your hotel?" she said.

"Absolutely," he said.

Chapter Thirteen

Nicolette drove and Justin navigated the route to his hotel. When they pulled into the lot Justin pointed to where Nicolette should park at a valet podium near the curb of the front of the hotel. It was the first and probably last time her beat-up little compact car would be treated to such a courtesy but what the hell. It was probably the first and last time she herself would check-in or visit such a nice hotel either. It was obvious Justin had a couple of bucks but he didn't act like it. If he did Nicolette wouldn't want to be there in the first place. Justin dressed modestly definitely with his own quirky, sometimes awkward, style. She liked it.

Once in the hotel, Nicolette noticed the people watching them almost staring as they made their way through the lobby and into the elevator. Justin moved closer to Nicolette and he looked as though he might push her against the wall and make love to her right there in the elevator but he didn't. Instead, he brushed his hand onto her hand accidentally on purpose. Nicolette mimicked the same motion back to him and they both grinned. She had never been with someone so confident yet also timid and shy. He showed her respect she had never experienced before. He didn't rush her or push himself on her he let her come to him. She was completely attracted to him and he to her. If he pulled back, she came forward. If he came forward, she pulled back. It was like they were strong magnets flipped towards the opposite sides but magnets just the same. Each time she felt the push and pull it made her mad with desire for him.

It seemed as if it took forever to get to the eighth floor but Nicolette finally being in close proximity to Justin it could have continued to ascend forever and that wouldn't have been long enough. Once off of the elevator Justin took Nicolette's hand in his. His hand was soft and steady, but his fingernails worn. She loved the way his fingers felt intertwined with hers. The anticipation of being with him was more exciting than anything she had ever wanted in her life. She put her other hand over his as if trying to hold on for dear life. They reached his door and he let go of her hand to get his room key out of his wallet. She studied his frame as he moved while biting her bottom lip. Nicolette stood nervously with one hand on her hip and twirled her hair with a finger on her other. The shape of his body titillated her from his arms to his firm round derriere on down to his oversized feet in extremely worn shoes. He was so unique. Different than anyone she had ever met.

"How long have you had those shoes?" she asked.

"Quite a while. I hate spending money on that stuff," he said.

Nicolette loved how he seemed to fit the cliché of someone dancing to their own beat although she believed their beats were identical in many ways. She had always felt like an outcast in crowds even if they were all friends of hers who knew her well and liked her. Suddenly with Justin, she felt a kindred spirit floating with her. He was somewhat carefree but at moments seemed to almost over-analyze small details. She was the same way. At the bar when she had dropped off his check, she recalled him commenting on how amazing it was the number of hands his transaction had to touch in order for him to merely swipe a plastic card and someone would bring him a meal. From his card to the restaurant and the credit card company to the bank for verification and back to the restaurant with approval. She marveled at the way his brain worked. Her brain understood him perfectly.

Justin pushed the door open and held it with his arm for Nicolette to go in first. He was such a gentleman. The room was like none she had stayed in before. It wasn't very big but the bed looked enormous and it had a big fancy tv and a sliding door that opened to a patio with flowing curtains around it. The bathroom had a door but separate shower room was enclosed by clear glass walls that could be seen from the bedroom if the curtains on the bedroom wall weren't drawn. The shower was bigger than the kitchen at her townhouse with tile ceiling and walls, a huge floor drain and a showerhead that was so large it looked like a UFO.

There was a loveseat with a coffee table in front of it and a small kitchenette with cabinets, a sink, stocked bar, microwave, and a mini-refrigerator directly across from it. An illuminated lamp on the side table exposed a still packed back-pack and what looked like a laptop bag neatly placed on the chair next to the patio door. The place didn't look lived in at all except for a half-empty bottle of tequila and a used plastic cup sitting next to a water bottle on the coffee table.

"Well this is home for the next few days," he said.

"Not too shabby," she said.

Justin put his cell phone and wallet into his backpack while Nicolette set her purse against the wall and took her place on the loveseat. Justin poured a small amount of tequila into the used plastic cup and offered Nicolette her own cup but she declined. He pulled an extra water bottle out of the mini-fridge and handed it to her before sitting down next to her on the love seat. Because of the intense attraction pulling their bodies together, Nicolette assumed they would have sex right away but they didn't. Instead, they talked and laughed for hours sharing stories from their lives. Nicolette's brain fired on all cylinders when she listened to Justin and her heart grew more attached to him the way he intently listened to her. She knew he could hear her because he didn't just sit quietly waiting for her to stop talking like Jamie did. Once she finished Justin had questions or interjected humor or a story of his own. She could tell he actually saw her. It made her excited and instantly frightened to like him too much in case he went away as all good things in her life seemed to.

Nicolette didn't have much trust or confidence to place in other people. Because of her past, it was in short supply. Justin seemed to smash through all of those barriers and leave her defenseless. She was falling in love with him immediately and that just didn't happen with her this strong. Jamie and she had rushed into their life together and it never felt like this. As magnetic as she thought it was with Jamie in the beginning, this fierce natural bond with Justin felt like home. Nicolette was so aroused by Justin and wanted to touch him. She reached over and took the plastic cup of tequila from his hand, took a sip and set in on the table.

"I am having trouble sitting next to you like this. You are so handsome," she said.

"You are pretty good looking yourself, young lady," he said.

Justin placed his hand on Nicolette to give her a sign he heard what she was saying.

"You can touch both of them. They are pretty much alike but you still can if you want," she said.

Justin leaned back and patted his stomach signaling for her to lay back next to him under her arm. She felt so safe there. His arm that was wrapped around her was comforting and he rubbed his hand firmly up and down her side waist and hip feeling her form. She tingled all over and loved how it felt to be near him. His natural scent was so erotic to her. Nicolette's hand brushed the front of his jeans and she could see him harden underneath them so she touched him there again on purpose to learn what he felt like. Desire welled up inside her and she turned and looked up at him. His head was back and his eyes closed but he opened them when she spoke.

"I want you," she said.

"I want you too," he said.

Their calm turned to a frenzy of flailing hands, removing glasses, clothing, and feeling each other's bodies. He was a timid kisser but his lips were as soft as they originally appeared and she loved the way he tasted. Nicolette took charge and stood up to pull off his jeans but left him in his boxer briefs. She straddled his lap and started grinding on him with no self-control. She was able to stop long enough to stand up and slowly pull down her slacks and drop them to the floor exposing her black and gold tanga panties. Before returning on top of him she pulled down his grey boxer briefs exposing his thick visually pleasing manhood and gently stroked it with her hand memorizing every vein and curve. Justin moaned as she felt him.

Nicolette was so wet beneath her panties and she climbed back up to straddle him once again. As she made hip circles on his lap and rubbed herself on top of him, she could feel him almost enter her through the thin nylon of her panties that served as the only barrier to their pleasure. To avoid having to climb off of him once more Nicolette pulled the crotch of her panties to the side to expose her wetness for him to touch. Justin reached down and positioned himself to enter her. When he plunged into her warmest place she moaned and leaned her mouth to his ear.

"Finally," she said.

The frenzy of kissing, touching and thrusting continued. Nicolette rubbed her fingers through his already tousled hair, kissed his neck and licked his flesh as Justin tasted hers. Justin stopped her and leaned her back on the love seat, kneeled to the floor, put a hand on each of her knees and parted them slowly. Nicolette was about to explode with anticipation as Justin carefully kissed and licked as he tasted her warm wetness between her thighs. His tongue was gentle but firm and very skillful.

"I am going to come," she said.

Justin said nothing he just reached up and caressed her breasts as he licked her to orgasm. After giving Nicolette a moment to regain some thought process he gently took her hand.

"Come with me," he said.

Justin led her to the bed where he sat on the edge and leaned back leaving his feet on the floor. She knew what he wanted. She felt the entirety of his body with her hands and grabbed his hard shaft in her hand. Some of her wetness was still on him and he glistened slightly. Nicolette wanted to taste him so badly and lowered her head down and took him in her mouth. His was so thick he filled her mouth and she could only move so far down on him before her mouth was full. She wanted to suck him until he came in her mouth but she wanted to feel him inside her more. Nicolette stood up near the side of the bed as Justin pulled himself all the way atop the bed to lay flat on his back. Nicolette pulled off her panties, threw them towards the chair and they landed on his backpack. She straddled him and feverishly lowered herself down on him. He reached so far inside her it felt like she was coming every time he moved. No one had ever made her feel that way before. It was almost an out of body experience. Nicolette couldn't help but ride him hard and fast she wanted him so much.

"Slow down or I am not going to last long," he said.

"I can't so you be in charge," she said.

Nicolette dismounted him and threw herself down on her back and spread her legs wide making it easy for him to flip over and enter her once more. Their bodies moved so naturally together and as Nicolette ground her hips and tightened the muscles inside her around his throbbing cock the change of positions proved to be futile. Nicolette rubbed his back and caressed his arms as he thrust towards her and deep inside her and she spoke softly.

"Come inside me," she said.

Justin immediately let go and came inside her. They both moaned in unison and clung to each other until their orgasms dissipated and the sexual fever wore off a little bit. Nicolette traced his hair, ears, shoulders and back with her fingers and rubbed her palms on his back so she would never forget the way he felt. His body would forever be imprinted in her memory for as long as she lived.

"Do you want to get in the shower with me?" he asked.

"Absolutely," she said.

They made their way to the bathroom and Justin turned on the water adjusting it to make sure it was just the correct temperature for them. He stepped into the water and then offered her hand leading her across the wet tile. The water was warm but not as hot as they were when they were near each other. As they drenched themselves in water and took turns soaping each other up, they caressed every inch of one another and shared passionate kisses while the water streamed down their faces, across their playful tongues, and down their bodies.

After drying off Nicolette hung her towel and Justin threw his over his shoulder. Justin gave Nicolette the extra toothbrush provided by the hotel and retrieved his from his bag. They stood naked by the bathroom sink looking at each other playfully as the toothpaste bubbled on their teeth and on their lips. Justin let Nicolette spit and rinse first and after his turn, he scooped up some water in the faucet and playfully tossed it at Nicolette. She playfully scolded him, ran out of the bathroom and jumped into the bed. As Justin approached the side of the bed, she watched him studying his shape and where the hair on his body was concentrated. Every inch of him even his now flaccid part. To her, he was the best-looking man in the world and wanted to look at him that way forever.

Nicolette pulled back the covers to invite Justin inside them. She snuggled up to his side and put her leg over his. Her breasts pushed up against the side of his chest and she reached around his hip trying to get a feel of his perfect round buttock. As she felt him, she became aroused again and pressed her pelvis towards him leaving her wetness on his thigh as she wiggled beside him, she reached down and touched him checking for renewed hardness. Nicolette discovered he was also becoming aroused so she inched herself down until her head disappeared under the covers and once again took him in her mouth. She felt him grow harder and harder against the back of her throat as she sucked on him like a popsicle. Her tongue swirled on the head of his penis like she was licking an ice cream cone but to her, he tasted sweeter than either of those. Nicolette could feel him tremble and heard his muffled moan through the blanket and sheet covering her.

Nicolette increased the speed and intensity of her mouth wrapped around him her hand stroking the bottom of his shaft as he exploded in her mouth. His legs tensed and his hands reached down to caress her hair leading her by her cheeks off of him and pulled her back up to lay beside him. He handed her his towel from the shower they shared which he had dropped next to the bed. Nicolette innocently wiped her lips with it. Justin reached over and pushed the button on the lamp beside the bed to turn it off. They laid still all but his hand that stroked her bangs away from her face. She listened to his heartbeat against her cheek until they both fell fast asleep.

Chapter Fourteen

In the morning when Nicolette opened her eyes, she was excited to realize she was still with Justin. It was the first time in quite a while she felt as if she'd slept hard. Also, the first time in a while she didn't have bad dreams. Instead of her usual waking up alone, she found herself with her cheek still pressed against Justin's chest and his arm still around her. They hadn't moved all night and as she reached up to wipe a tiny spot of drool from her lip and Justin's chest he started to move. He opened his eyes and said good morning in a sweet groggy voice as if just as happy to see her as she was him.

"Do you want some coffee? Are you a breakfast eater?" he asked.

"I would love some coffee and yes I could eat. I am famished," she said.

Justin picked up the phone and called down to room service while Nicolette disappeared into the restroom to get rid of her morning breath with a second teeth brushing and use the restroom. Nicolette kept bursting into uncontrollable smiles as she welled up with a joy she had never felt before. When she was finished, she returned to the bed where Justin still laid. He was gorgeous and she still couldn't believe he was really there. Nicolette jumped on the bed and gave Justin a peck on the cheek.

"Ooh minty," he said.

"I should go do the same for you," he said.

Justin popped up off the bed looking rested and suddenly full of energy as he made his way to the bathroom and shut the door behind him. A couple of minutes passed and there was a knock at the door. Nicolette dashed to the door and looked out the peek hole to see it was room service with a rolling cart carrying two silver covered plates and other items. She quickly threw her clothes back on from the night before since it was all she had. Minus the panties of course because she couldn't remember where she had flung them. Nicolette opened the door and held it wide so the man could roll the cart in and stop it near the coffee table.

"Is this fine here Mrs. Bend?" he asked.

"Oh, I am not…" she started.

"Yes, that is just fine thank you," she said.

The man paused for a moment as if he was waiting for Nicolette to do something. She had never had room service before so she didn't really know what she was supposed to do next and she stood there awkward and unaware.

"Let Mr. Bend know we will charge it to his room no problem," he said.

Nicolette glanced for the nametag on the front of the man's jacket. She preferred to call people by their first names if she knew what they were.

"Thank you, Steven," she said.

"You are welcome, Mam," he said.

Steven showed himself out of the room as Nicolette spun in circles as if she was wearing the most beautiful flowing dress known to man. She pictured it twirling high up to her waist as any good dress should and when she stopped it wrapped itself around her hip and fell back down toward the floor. Justin came out of the restroom just in time to catch her last spin. Normally she would have been embarrassed but she felt so comfortable with him she wasn't at all. Nicolette smiled at him and wrapped her arms around his neck and kissed him passionately.

"Mmmm minty," she said.

His finger traced the slight bump on the bridge of her nose and he kissed it on the tip. He looked her straight in the eyes. He really saw her. Her nose was the feature she possessed which she was the most insecure about and he seemed to take all of that away with his touch.

"You are so beautiful," he said.

"So are you," she said.

Justin was still buck naked. As Nicolette approached the cart to serve them the food at the love seat and coffee table Justin stopped her and he sarcastically waved her up and down signaling his disapproval for her having to get dressed to answer the door.

"Wait a minute. You need to take those back off and get back in bed, I will do the serving. Nicolette gladly took all of her clothes back off and strewn them about the floor on her way to launch herself back into the bed screeching like a child on Christmas morning. She scooted to one side to make room for Justin and sat up leaned back against the pillows with the blanket pulled up to her waist and waited patiently while he served her. He placed the tray holding the two silver covered plates, linen-wrapped silverware, condiments, two cups of coffee, and a large orange juice down in front of her on the bed. He gently climbed in beside to her trying not to spill the beverages as he positioned himself next to her.

"I didn't know what you liked so I got a little of everything," he said.

Justin lifted the lids off of the trays and revealed what he had chosen for them. Nicolette added some cream to her coffee and stirred with a spoon as she marveled at how delicious the food looked and fascinated by Justin's choices. One plate was scrambled eggs, bacon, sausage, and hash browns. The other was a large crepe stuffed full of cream cheese and perfectly ripened strawberries and blueberries squishing out the ends. Justin handed her the cruet of freshly whipped cream in case she wanted to top it so she assumed he liked it too and dumped it over the top. The heat melting it a bit and surrounding the plate. There was a spare whipped cream on the tray she guessed in case the one wasn't enough.

Nicolette unwrapped her fork, cut a bite of the crepe, and turned to feed it to Justin. When his mouth parted to take in the fork full of food Nicolette tingled with desire for him. She now knew exactly what those lips and tongue were capable of. A tinge of jealousy towards the crepe made her giggle as he pulled it into his mouth. Justin took his fork and returned Nicolette's kindness by feeding her. She picked up a sausage link with her fingers and offered it to him.

"No thank you I don't eat meat," he said.

"Ok. Well, I do. I am a carnivore," she said.

Nicolette acted like a savage when she bit into the link and growled at him, and showed her teeth with the meat hanging out of them. Justin laughed and took a swipe full of cream with his index finger from the crepe and put it to Nicolette's mouth. She took his finger in between her lips, tickled it with her tongue, and sucked it slowly the way she did his body when her head was buried under the covers the night before. They seductively fed each other bites of breakfast until they were both full. Nicolette loved the way they shared the same glass of juice. Everything they did together felt raw and intimate and oh so right. Justin set the extra cruet of whipped cream down on the bed and carried the tray back to the cart and returned to her side. He helped Nicolette recline so she was laying on her back. Justin carefully slid the covers down past her toes revealing her naked body in the sunlight. The rays were warm on her. He paused to take inventory of her shape.

Without saying a word, he picked up the cream and scooped some upon his finger. He swiped the first bit on her hip and sucked it off of her skin. The next one on her belly button. It tickled when he licked it with the tip of his tongue and Nicolette wiggled around. He worked his way to her breasts sucking cream off of each of her nipples slowly. He painted the next bit on her lips like he was a painter and she filled with desire as his tongue carefully erased it and plunged into her mouth. He made his way back down her body, parted her legs causing her to instantly get moist. Justin set the cruet back on the bed and place his finger between her thighs and applied the cream. He was as skillful as he was the night before.

Nicolette stopped him after he savored her sweetness for a few minutes. Traded places with him and grabbed the cruet in her hand. He was rock hard by then so she took what little bit of cream was left and covered him there. Nicolette thought he tasted sweet on his own without the cream but this time he was literally as sweet as ice cream. Once she had licked off all of the cream, she mounted him and they enjoyed each other thrusting and grinding until they came together. Nicolette's back arched, they both moaned, and collapsed on the bed satisfied.

"If I am going to stay, I really need to run home and get some clothes," she said.

"Do you want me to go with you or would you rather go alone?" he asked.

Jamie instantly came to mind like a harsh bolt of lightning for the first time since she arrived there with Justin. It gave her a twisted feeling in the pit of her stomach. She knew she had to tell Justin about him at some point if they were going to continue seeing each other but she wasn't certain how serious their relationship would turn out to be. Maybe Justin just wanted a fling. Nicolette couldn't see how that was possible for such a beautiful man who stepped out of her premonition and into her life would be anything less than her soul mate. Her life was never that easy though so no matter how great he was her pessimistic voice in her head told her there is no way she could deserve it.

Nicolette over-thought things and erred on the side of caution out of fear most of the time. She told herself it was quite possibly the inevitable destruction of every good thing that came along in her in life was a mixture of her worthlessness and products of self-fulfilling prophecies created out of fear. Nicolette wasn't ready to let the knowledge of Jamie ruin her time with Justin so she decided to avoid the topic until their weekend together was over.

"No thank you. It won't take me long. My place is only a few miles away. I will just run home and take a quick shower to get this fabulous stickiness off, grab some clothes, and be back in a jiffy," she said.

Justin reacted well to her quirky and corny sayings. He used them too. Nicolette tossed her clothes back on, again without her panties where ever they were and lingered at the door for a moment. Justin gave her another passionate kiss before hiding his nakedness behind the open door as she left. He stuck his head out the door to watch her go.

"Oh, and make sure you wear something good for hiking. I have somewhere I want to take you," he said.

As Nicolette drove, she was in another world as she reminisced about the events that had taken place since Justin was seated at her table at the bar. She was lucky she made it directly home without making a wrong turn with her distracting thoughts. Nicolette was again moist inside her slacks. Since Justin entered her life, she had been in a constant state of arousal even only moments after they had sex and every minute in between.

Nicolette unlocked the townhouse door and entered carefully. Jamie's vehicle wasn't in the lot and she wondered if he had even bothered to come home that night. Her suspicion was that he hadn't. There didn't seem to be anything moved or different since the day before when she left for work. The caller ID box didn't register any calls. Keres had stopped her obsessive calling the last few weeks for some reason. Maybe she found a life outside of harassing them finally. Nicolette wasn't sure what the change was but it was a welcomed one.

Nicolette showered, got dressed, and packed a bag to take back to the hotel. She put on some makeup and left her blown dry hair down around her shoulders but slid a hair tie onto her wrist for later if she needed it, headed back out the front door to return to the hotel. The car didn't seem to go fast enough and she was impatient to get back to Justin. As she passed by the taco stand landmark once used to find her way around, she was stopped by the stoplight. Whilst she waited her eyes glanced around at the few cars surrounding her that were stopped too. Nicolette scanned the taco stand sign and the small outside seating area. There was one couple holding hands across the table leaning into each other as they spoke. They looked familiar to her but from the distance, she wasn't quite sure. One scan of the taco stand parking lot and she saw Jamie's car and then Keres's. Her eyes darted back towards the couple at the table as the traffic light turned green for her and the cars around her began to move pulling her with them. She wrenched her neck to keep her eyes connected to the couple and she knew it was them. Lulu was not there that she could see.

Anger welled up inside her. Nicolette wondered if this is why Keres no longer called obsessively. She and Jamie had obviously found other ways to communicate. If Nicolette had any guilt for spending time with Justin it was gone at that moment. Strangely it was almost more of a relief for Nicolette to see Jamie and Keres together, at least after the initial sting of her discovery. It suddenly opened up a freedom Nicolette hadn't felt since she and Jamie rushed into merging their lives together. Most of her time was spent taking care of his responsibilities he didn't have time for or was too lazy to do. She didn't feel very appreciated and on the contrary often blamed for everything that went wrong. Especially everything Jamie did wrong.

Nicolette pulled into the hotel and purposefully cleared her mind of any thoughts of Jamie and Keres. Maybe if they got back together it would be good for Lulu to have both of her parents in one place again even if they were terrible together. Maria sure wasn't going to like it but that was her brother's fault, not Nicolette's and that was the end of her worrying about it. Nicolette grabbed her freshly packed bag, hurried into the hotel, and back to her literal and figurative dream man. Justin was clean and dressed with some moisture left in the few curls of his hair that hung past his ears. He was dressed in shorts and a t-shirt and the same black and white well-worn sneakers he had on when she met him. He was even more handsome than when she left him last if that was possible.

Justin took her to a small mountainous area on the outskirts of town. The scenery was mostly wide-open space and rock platforms with hiking trails that lead up and down and around bends. Clusters of trees were in various places along the way. They took a path that led down to a somewhat secluded area next to a small pond. They hadn't encountered anyone else on their way. The two of them were bantering the whole way flirtatious and playful taking opportunities to examine each other's bodies as they walked and even some touchy-feely stuff when they stopped for a breath.

As they gazed holding hands side by side at the water's edge Justin took Nicolette in his arms to kiss her and he backed her up carefully until Nicolette was pressed against a tree and couldn't go further. Their kissing quickly turned to passion and Nicolette

dropped to her knees, pulled his elastic-waisted

athletic shorts down just far enough to take him in her

mouth. She couldn't get enough of him. Justin guided

her up to her feet, gently turned her around and she

leaned forward placing both palms on the tree trunk

for stability as he slid her shorts and pink laced

panties down just far enough to enter her from

behind.

It didn't take Nicolette much time to come with

Justin. He made sure she was satisfied every time.

Her sex life with Jamie had gone stale and it seemed

like he just used her when he was horny because she

was there but he wasn't an attentive lover and she was

left disgruntled, pent up, and disappointed most of the

time. After seeing him at the taco stand earlier that

day she wondered if she now knew why. At least one

of the reasons maybe. They also really had nothing in common anymore. Nicolette was dreamy and romantic. Jamie was often cold and harsh. It seemed like any joy Nicolette expressed was greeted by him with his immediate need to knock her down a few pegs. Her elation often turned to tears, anger or both within minutes.

Justin and Nicolette quickly pulled their clothes back on and finished their hike holding hands the whole way. Nicolette loved how enamored Justin was with the scenery and the animals they encountered. He seemed to see the beauty and artistic nature of everything around them just like Nicolette did. Justin seemed to always have a tune in his head he would hum, likely because of his job. He unlocked a whole new part of Nicolette she didn't know existed but somehow, she knew it always had. It was just beaten down after years of dealing with other people's issues. When they took their anger or perversion out on her it seemed to stifle and mask the true parts of who she was. She felt more like a receptacle for their discarded waste than a human being. Justin single-handedly unlocked the door inside her where all of the wonder, creativity and optimistic free spirit lived, and gently handed her the key.

Chapter Fifteen

On the way back to the hotel Justin took Nicolette to an amazing vegetarian restaurant she had never been to before. He had only been there once a couple of years ago when he was in town briefly for a show. It looked like a house or a bait shop like the ones back in her hometown and it sat at the corner lot just outside of a residential area across town. It had wooden steps that led up to a wraparound deck with a mixture of umbrella and picnic tables placed about. There was a long line of people waiting to get in. When they got close enough to the front door, they scanned the walls. They were covered in multiple handwritten menu items on marker boards. Apparently, they had vegan options. Nicolette wasn't sure what the difference was between vegetarian and vegan. Justin explained it to her without hesitation or judgment for her not knowing already.

Nicolette had a teacher once who told her, "The only stupid question is a question not asked." That statement stuck with Nicolette. She carried it with her throughout her life and reminded herself of it when she was in a situation where she felt insecure about not knowing an answer to a certain subject. Although she recognized it as a possibly useful skill in some circumstances, Nicolette was never a fan of people who bullshitted their way through subjects trying to be an expert they knew nothing about. She did, however, appreciate creating over the top stories about people she watched in public. Nicolette would animate their voices and treat them like actors in her own play but only if everyone knew it was satire. Justin had that skill too but he was far from a bullshitter about the things he didn't know. He had lived a lot of life and Nicolette had yet to hear something he didn't at least have a bit of experience with and she respected that.

When it was their time to order Nicolette settled on a spinach tortilla wrap filled with grilled portobello mushroom and onion, melted mozzarella cheese, and a sun-dried tomato drizzle. Justin followed her lead and ordered the same. They sat out on the sunny patio eating the amazing food and enjoying the conversation. Nicolette loved how easy it was to get to know him. He had no boundary he wouldn't let her cross and they were both free to be who they were. They seemed to match perfectly and Nicolette fell deeper and deeper in love with him.

When they finished their food, they sat for a moment soaking up the last of the sun rays as it lowered from the sky. It was the first time either of them mentioned Justin having to leave town early the morning after next to get back to work. He had a tour coming up out of the country and there would be lots of travel and a busy schedule for several months. Nicolette's heart sank at the thought of saying goodbye to him but she didn't ruin the mood by telling him. They discussed how they would be able to keep in close contact while he was gone.

On the way back to the hotel Justin stopped by a local pop-up phone store and purchased Nicolette her first cell phone as a gift. Remarkably he actually saw it as a gift for himself to get to stay in contact with her and be there when she needed him, the best he could be anyway. He helped her program the first number into it. It, of course, was his. They stopped by a liquor store and Justin grabbed another bottle of his favorite tequila, a bottle of Riesling for her, and a deck of some kind of cards he wouldn't show to Nicolette.

They were both happily exhausted from the day and eager to get back to the hotel to relax. Once inside the door, Justin collapsed on the love seat and placed the tequila and wine on the table but he still wouldn't show her the cards. Nicolette told Justin she was going to freshen up and asked him to get a bucket of ice to chill her wine because she liked her Riesling nice and cold and he agreed. Nicolette took her bag she had packed into the bathroom and closed the door behind her, used the facilities and stripped down naked. She peeked into the shower room and contemplated a shower. The curtains were closed on the opposite side of the glass wall so the view from the room into the shower was obstructed. Nicolette started the shower and turned it up as steamy and hot as she could stand. She had some dirt from the hike on her legs and ankles and a few scratches from branches too. As she started to lather herself with the bar of soap, she could tell the water was pure and made her skin feel so soft. The last shower she had taken in that room was with Justin so she was too distracted to notice. After having a shower at her place earlier that day she could tell the obvious contrast between the hard and soft water.

As she closed her eyes and washed her hair with the luxurious smelling shampoo, she heard a soft motor sound and turned to look as the curtains were slowly opening on the other side of the glass exposing her to anyone watching on the other side. Since the size of the shower room was fairly large the steam dissipated enough so she could still see Justin clearly on the other side as he sat back down on the love seat and watched her. Nicolette could see her wine chilling in a bucket and Justin leaned back sipping on his glass of tequila neat with his arm up and palm resting on the back of his neck. His eyes were intense with desire and a small grin curled at the corners of his mouth.

Nicolette felt compelled to do a momentary slow dance for him near the glass. It was part humorous like everything she did but innocently seductive at the same time. Justin never joined her he just watched her and sipped his tequila as she washed and rinsed herself. When she turned off the water and grabbed her towel from the wall, he hollered a playful boo through the glass and it made her laugh.

Nicolette brushed her hair and put the sides up in clips instead of blow it dry. Knowing they were likely in for the evening, she slipped on her favorite short black flowing A-line nightgown but skipped the panties and the makeup. The nightgown only came down mid-thigh but the hem was flowing and loose enough to twirl like a fantastic dress.

When she left the bathroom to rejoin Justin at the love seat he broke into applause when she came around the corner and into his sight. God, he made her feel special and alive. Everything about him was attractive to her and it was easy for time to disappear when she was in his presence. Justin poured a glass of wine and handed it to Nicolette as she took her place beside him. She motioned towards the empty shower room through the glass and challenged him.

"Your turn," she said.

"I think that is a great idea. I am spent," he said.

Nicolette had a sense of pride that their time had worn him out the way it had. They both were so relaxed at this point and as comfortable as a favorite pair of jeans feels on your body. Justin made a few silly gestures as he entered the shower room but otherwise, he just got lost in the comfort of his shower. Nicolette loved the playful and sexy side of him but for some reason, nothing was sexier than to just watch him through the glass caring for his hair and soaping his body as if she wasn't watching. Nicolette felt true happiness for the first time in her life.

When Justin came out of the shower, he was in just a pair of boxer briefs and his hair looked towel-dried and still perfect to Nicolette. They finished their drinks and decided on a movie to crawl into bed and watch together. Nicolette loved the way his body felt when she was pressed up against him. Justin played some beautiful music in his career but for Nicolette to feel his breath and listen to his heartbeat was the best music of all. The sun had barely finished going down and most people were probably just making plans to go out somewhere to socialize for the night. But at that moment in time, in that tiny slice of heaven on earth, they were still, holding each other, and didn't get too far into the movie before they both fell asleep.

Nicolette woke up alone to the sound of a cell phone notification bell with her face buried in a pillow. She looked around the room and saw Justin at the foot of the bed, his face illuminated by the light of the phone. He noticed her move and smiled warmly when their eyes met.

"Sorry. I just got the itinerary for my travel plans coming up in…" he started.

Justin looked down at his phone and did some quick math in his head.

"Well I guess realistically about twenty-four hours from now," he finished.

Nicolette looked at the clock and it was just after twenty-one-hundred. She had learned to calculate military time from a couple of friends with military experience. Since they always used it in their letters when they wrote she felt it necessary to learn and it became second nature to her.

"I thought you still had another night here tomorrow?" she asked.

"Yeah I did but unfortunately that flight was canceled and they had to move me up to one for tomorrow night. Part of the biz," he said.

For a moment Nicolette thought she caught a glimpse of the life that Justin led when he wasn't held up in a hotel with a stranger for a few days off. Nicolette felt her automatic defenses begin to rebuild themselves just a little. She didn't like the feeling and fought hard against it. It was important to her for whatever time they had left to try and stay open and vulnerable like she had been with him and not fall back into her hiding place. It wasn't his fault the flight was canceled. This kind of thing happens in life and she told herself she just had to try not to be sensitive, just accept it, and enjoy their next twenty-four hours together best she could.

"I understand," she said.

But she didn't.

Nicolette rose from the bed and kissed Justin softly on his lips as she passed by before wandering over towards the sliding glass door. She threw the curtains wide open revealing the view of the night sky and the lights of the town. It looked different up that high. Justin came up behind her and hugged her with his hands around her waist and rested his chin on her shoulder while they shared the view. She turned to him and they kissed passionately with her hands wrapped around the nape of his neck. They both were distracted by each other and left the curtains wide. The light from the lamp on the side table reflected off of the glass.

Justin poured Nicolette another glass of wine and of course, he a tequila, neat. He went to the kitchenette and retrieved the cards he had bought earlier hidden in the cabinet and brought them back to where she was standing. He hopped onto the bed and sat cross-legged motioning for her to join him. Nicolette sat cross-legged directly across from him; their knees touching. Justin removed the deck of cards from the pack, handed the instructions to Nicolette, and shuffled them as he watched her read the instructions aloud. The deck was called *He and She Cards.* The instructions were basic and simple. There were "he" and "she" cards with three levels. All they had to do was take turns turning over their card and do what it said for sixty seconds. It looked as though the rules might get a little intense by the look of the flames on the level three stack. Both were suddenly struck with butterflies and a hint of arousal. Justin wanted to peek at the cards in the stack just to see what lay ahead but Nicolette vetoed that suggestion.

"No peeking!" she said.

After Justin organized the stacks as directed. A coin toss decided Nicolette would go first. She drew her first card and read aloud.

"Male turns back to female while female writes secret messages on male's back," she said.

Nicolette decided to read it again and plug in their actual names so it was clearer to both of them.

"Justin turns back to Nicolette while Nicolette writes secret messages on Justin's back," she said.

Thankfully the first one was rather tame. Justin turned around on the bed and set his phone timer to sixty seconds. Nicolette raised her finger to his back and started to write. It felt amazing to Justin and exciting to Nicolette. Justin started to narrate out loud what he wanted her to be writing.

"Let's drop this game and I will fuck your brains out," he said.

They both laughed and she swatted his back lightly signaling it was likely something more innocuous but wouldn't tell him what it was. The timer beeped and Justin turned back around to draw his card. He took her cue and inserted names where the genders were.

"Justin give Nicolette a light massage of her hands and fingers. All eyes closed. Do not wander up the arm," he said.

Justin worked slowly around all of her fingers at first like a usual massage but the rhythm and feel took on a more desirous vibe as he continued. Nicolette breathed a little heavier from his touch when the phone alarm sounded. Sixty seconds was seeming extremely brief. They retained composure but with some mutual blushing. They continued through the stack of level one cards with various instructions of staring into each other's eyes and some harmless massage and places to touch. All of it was barely the first base level.

Stack one was completed and Nicolette got up to freshen her wine along with Justin's tequila and they were on to stack two. It was Nicolette's turn.

"Standing, Nicolette take Justin in full frontal embrace should slip her hands into the back of Justin's trousers beneath his underwear to feel and tease his derriere," she said.

Since Justin was only wearing boxer briefs at that point Nicolette complied but it was easier to get to him than the card suggested. They both giggled a bit as they stood to get into position and also at the word derriere. They blushed a little more. Justin visibly enjoyed Nicolette slipping her hands into his waistband and wandering them about his ass feeling the skin on skin. His throbbing shaft was now impossible to deny and it pressed against Nicolette's leg. It made her instantly wet. Sixty seconds felt like one.

Justin cleared his throat and Nicolette smiled wide as they sat back down for him to draw the next card.

"Justin face Nicolette with her eyes closed. Justin lightly massages Nicolette's breasts through her shirt with palms only with no fingers or any other touching," he said.

Justin wasn't ready for the energy he felt through her black nightgown. His cock was now pounding and it was torture. They continued through the instructions. Each duty was tougher to perform within the sixty-second timer. Nicolette drew another card.

"Nicolette turn on a porn movie of her choice. Justin and Nicolette sit with legs touching and watch. No speaking or any other touching," she said.

"Should we pass on this one?" she asked.

"We? What do you mean we? If you don't do it, I get my point," he said.

"Fine," she said.

Nicolette navigated the hotel television through all kinds of complicated menus with bad music and ads until she found the late-night viewing menu. She reluctantly pressed the button to accept the room charge for the crappy scenario about a sexy stepmom. The timer was set and they sat with legs touching as a montage of every position known to the human race played at an incredibly quick cut edge with terrible production value and even worse music. A bad set up scene with a student who looked at least thirty-five and his supposed porn stepmom who also looked thirty-five had only just started when they were saved by the bell. Luckily the first sixty seconds of a porn movie doesn't really go anywhere. The movie was left on in the background as they continued the game.

Level two was getting more torturous with minutes of neck kissing and massages through clothing. The only skin revealing one was Justin having to run his nose down Nicolette's back. In the background, the movie played on. They could both hear the awful dialogue and music. They moved on to level three and Nicolette drew her first card.

"Justin lay on his back, undo belt, zippers, and buttons for easy access. Leave underwear on while Nicolette massages Justin's cock through his underwear with hands or mouth," she said.

'They really like the word cock," she quipped.

They both laughed for a second but it dissipated quickly from their anticipation and a mutual increase of heart rate. Justin laid on his back on the bed, started the timer, and waited. Nicolette dutifully left his underwear in place but cupped him slightly with her hand through the fabric. Justin took a deep breath and let out a slightly nervous laugh that was quickly overcome by a whimpering sigh. Her touch was so gentle and sure he though if it were more than sixty seconds, she might bring him to come through his underwear.

In the background, the porno had ratcheted up a notch. The timer went off but Nicolette didn't stop. The game wasn't fun anymore. Nicolette wanted him inside her. She removed her black nightgown revealing her bareness with no panties and positioned herself up on her knees atop the bed with her back towards Justin. He reached around her with his hands on her thighs and it tickled her a bit. He pressed one finger inside her and then two. He moved them slowly and deliberately in and out of her as her wetness increased. Nicolette moaned and squirmed in his hands. His hardness was pressing on her from behind. They both caught their reflections in the glass of the sliding patio door. Nicolette arched her back and leaned her mouth to his ear.

"Fuck me. I want you to fuck me. Please put your cock inside me now!" she said.

Justin scrambled to remove his boxer briefs. The timer continued to sound as he entered her and thrust inside her as if both feeling desperate it may be the last time, at least for a while, they would get to be together. The woman's voice in the movie blaring from the television set was wailing and you could hear skin slapping and funk music in the background which normally would have made them both laugh hysterically.

When Justin heard the woman yell, "Oh my God I am coming! I am Coming! I am going to fucking come all over you, he couldn't help the feeling coming over his entire belly and thighs. It was an orgasm rising out of control. He called out to Nicolette for the first time since they had been together.

"Oh my God Nicolette I am going to come! I am going to come so hard inside you!" he said.

He did. It unleashed a quivering in Nicolette and they both shout-moaned together in a release that lasted at least the game timer length before they collapsed to the bed still intertwined.

"Who draws the next card?" he asked.

They were both too tired to laugh.

Chapter Sixteen

Nicolette woke to the sounds of thunder and flashes of lightning blazing through the hotel windows. She glanced at the clock and it was only o-six-thirty. Neither her nor Justin closed the curtains the night before out of sheer exhaustion. Justin was still asleep. She could feel his warm breath softly exhale on the back of her neck. His arms were still wrapped around her from behind as she watched and waited for the lightning strikes through the panes on the door and counted how long it was in between the flash and the thunder. One one-thousand, two one-thousand. She had learned that by watching a movie one time with some friends. Something about a little girl, a television set and some tennis balls or something. She couldn't remember exactly how the movie went but she distinctly remembered by the end of it a house was clean and she had a new knack to for telling the distance of how far away a storm was.

The room was silent and the energy was different than it was since the beginning of her stay. The warmth and comfort once exuded by the walls were tinged with lingering loneliness trying to seep in. Nicolette's thoughts drifted away from counting distance to counting the hours she had left with Justin. She began to ponder what the best way for them to spend them was but couldn't come up with anything that didn't sound sad. Thoughts of their imminent goodbye clouded any good scenarios she could think of. Nicolette started to feel her old friend pessimism settle into her mind for a visit. It wasn't welcome but she was virtually powerless against it once it came to call. Like a terrible house guest, once it entered the door, sat on her mind's sofa, and put its feet up she was never certain when it would pack up and go. Nicolette sat still and silent.

Justin's head flew off his pillow when the alarm on his phone went off and startled Nicolette. He jerked his arm out from under Nicolette allowing her head to abruptly bounce back down on the pillow. She turned to him with a look of confusion in her eyes and sat up.

"Is everything okay?" she asked.

"Sorry Nic I got to go," he said.

"Wait what? It is early. I didn't think your plane left until tonight?" she said.

"You don't understand my schedule and just how busy I always am. My days off are few and far between. It is not your fault, no one understands," he said.

"Ok. Do you want me to order us some breakfast while you shower?" she asked.

"Aww thanks, Nic. I don't have time but it has been fun. My manager is coming with the van to get me. Something about press interviews or something. I never really pay attention to it. I just show up when they tell me too. Well, most of the time," he said.

Nicolette sat up in the bed confused watching Justin collect what few things he had strewn about the place. He tossed his bags on the foot of the bed and scrambled around for his phone and clothing that were strewn about. Nicolette glanced back at the chair his bags had been sitting on and spotted the pair of black and gold tanga panties she'd lost track of the first night, reached over, and grabbed them. She twisted them in her fingers trying to make sense of the quick exit Justin was making.

When he disappeared into the bathroom for a moment Nicolette stuffed her panties into one of his bags to send a part of her with him. Justin returned to the bedside and gave her two quick and awkward kisses that missed her mouth slightly and grabbed his bags. He paused for just a moment as he threw his bag over his shoulder.

"Thanks for the hang. You're a good egg Nic," he said.

Nicolette was stunned by the change in his demeanor and couldn't muster a response. Justin turned and went to the door, he looked back and waved as he disappeared into the hallway. As the door slowly closed behind him, she heard his muffled voice.

"Catch you on the flip side," he said.

Nicolette still sat stunned. After a few moments, she unfroze slightly and glanced around the room at the remnants of their time together as tears rolled down her cheeks. Nicolette placed her palms over her face and eyes and hung her head in disappointment. The room became dark and started to close in on her. Fear set in quickly. She threw herself back against her pillow and pulled the covers up over her face to hide from it as she did when she was a child.

The thunder crashed and Nicolette jumped. Justin jumped too. Nicolette was also startled when she realized Justin still had his arm firmly wrapped around her waist. She must have been dreaming. Her emotions were conflicted still filled with the sadness from what she quickly dubbed a nightmare in contrast to the warmth of his presence. His hand began to rub on her skin to comfort her as he brought it from her side to her shoulder and swiped her hair back exposing her neck. Justin planted his warm lips first on her shoulder and then on her neck.

"Good morning beautiful," he said.

Nicolette said nothing. She turned to him, stared directly in his eyes and tears began to fall down her face and onto the pillow. Justin pulled her closer to him and did his best to wipe them away with his hand. His heartbeat raced loudly in her ear.

"It is okay Nicolette. I don't want to go either," he said.

"Then don't," she said.

"Unfortunately, that isn't the way it works. I have people who count on me. Employees and obligations.

Don't worry we will figure all of this stuff out. Trust me," he said.

Nicolette perked up when she heard the word trust. No one had ever asked that of her before, at least with actual words. It was something people just silently expected from her whether they deserved it or not. She tried to give trust freely like a neatly wrapped gift but so far anytime she had it was returned to her bruised, battered, and usually beaten to a pulp.

"Look, let's get cleaned up and packed. Check out is in a couple of hours. Doesn't your place open soon? Let's go have one of those flatbread veggie pizzas and a beer or two. It was pretty damn good the other night actually," he said.

Nicolette still sat quietly but watched closely as he spoke to her. She nodded in agreement at his proposed plan.

"You take the first shower. I will call my manager and have them swing by the Rusty Spur around two o'clock to pick me up," he said.

"But I thought your plane didn't leave until nine?" she asked.

"It does but there is a press interview that got squeezed in at the last minute. It happens sometimes. Also, it's better for us to get to the airport and checked in early rather than late, especially for international flights," he said.

"Okay. That makes sense," she said.

"It will be okay Nicolette. Just breathe," he said.

"I will Justin. Thank you," she said.

Justin leaned in and kissed her long and slow. Neither cared about morning breath or anything other than wanting to be close to each other. Nicolette couldn't remember anyone who ever before comforted her when she cried the way Justin did. Even as a child her tears seemed to drive people away or stay and yell at her to stop, the way her Dad did; the way Jamie did. She had never compared the two in her mind before and she suddenly realized it wasn't the only similarity between Jamie and Stan.

Nicolette closed the curtain on the wall before going in to take her shower. She felt more cautious and had a sense of needing to guard herself in order to get through the next couple of hours. After she got dressed, did her makeup and dried her hair, she gathered her things from the bathroom and put them back into her bag. Nicolette pulled the hair tie from her wrist and put her hair up as she often did, looked herself in the mirror, and took a deep breath.

When she came back into the room where Justin was, he stood, still naked as he pulled out his clothes he intended to wear after his shower and packed everything else back in his bag. He picked up the black and gold tanga panties Nicolette had misplaced that had gotten stuck between the arm and cushion of the chair. He spun them on his index finger and smiled as he brought them to his nose and breathed in deep.

"Can I keep these? They still smell like us?" he asked.

Nicolette burst into laughter and it felt like such a relief.

"Yes, of course, you can Mr. Bend," she said.

Justin showered and dressed. They both took a few passes through the room to make sure they hadn't forgotten anything and made their way downstairs to the front lobby. Nicolette stood with their bags as she watched Justin talking to the man behind the counter. He was so genuine, charismatic and kind. Everyone seemed to like him. Nicolette sure did. Her heart sank as she watched him give back the room key and let them know they were checking out. She wanted to grab his hand, run back upstairs, lock the door to the outside world, and stay there with him forever. The looming reality was telling her loud and clear that she couldn't.

They put their things in Nicolette's car and headed off to the Rusty Spur. The rest of their time together wasn't fluid but happened in snapshots. They were seated at the same table Justin had sat alone in the night they met. Flatbread pizza and beers were served. They sat outside on the bench as the rain drizzled off the awning overhead waiting for a van to pick Justin up. They stood in the rain, kissed and hugged each other goodbye while Nicolette tried to hold on to him for dear life. Nicolette sat on the bench alone in the rain paralyzed by the fact he was gone. She stayed for a while as the rain increased in intensity fearful to walk to her car and leave the bench behind. Nicolette was terrified if she got into her car and went back home Justin would leave her behind.

The deafening silence was broken when Maria came out of the front door of the bar, rushed towards Nicolette, sat beside her, threw her arms around her and held her tight. Nicolette loved Maria but her embrace felt empty but only because she wasn't Justin.

"Are you okay sweetie? What happened? Jamie has been calling me nonstop trying to find you. I haven't heard from him yet today though," she said.

Oh yeah, Jamie. Nicolette didn't respond to Maria. She just sobbed in her arms for a few moments before forcing a stoic composure.

"I am sorry. I have to go," Nicolette said.

"It's totally okay, sweetie. Call me when you are ready to talk," Maria said.

Nicolette walked robotically to her car in the rain as if she couldn't feel it soaking her down and drenching her clothes. She didn't care. Nicolette started the car and headed towards the townhouse and back to her old life.

When she came in the front door, she noticed Jamie wasn't there, as usual. She placed the half-empty bottle of wine on the counter and poured a glass to finish it off so she could bury the bottle in the trash and not have to explain it to Jamie if he came home. With her bag on her shoulder, a wine glass in one hand, and the nearly full bottle of Tequila Justin couldn't take with him in the other, she started towards the stairwell to go up and put her things away. On her way past the phone she noticed the caller ID box blinking blue and leaned to see, there were the max twenty-five calls registered just like old times. Nicolette didn't care. She didn't stop and made her way upstairs to the bedroom.

Nicolette set her glass of wine on the desk, threw her bag on the bed and hid the tequila in a desk drawer. It wasn't as if she really had to hide neither the wine nor Justin's tequila from Jamie. It wasn't uncommon for there to be alcohol in the house. It was more as if

Nicolette was hiding memories of Justin in a drawer so she didn't have to look at them. The ones in her head were hard enough to control. Her emotions they evoked she would have to learn to tame or they were going to drive her insane. Nicolette sipped her wine as she put away the clean things from her bag and her makeup and other personal items back into the bathroom.

As she made a pile of dirty clothes to take down to the laundry room, she remembered her missing panties now safely in Justin's possession. She thought of how he sniffed them and asked to keep them and it made her smile. The smile quickly turned to tears. Nicolette collapsed on the bed wiping her tears from her cheeks. Her thoughts drifted to their stay at the hotel. Visions of their naked bodies colliding and flailing hands and tongues exploring flesh. Her hand slid down her front, under her jeans, and into her panties. Nicolette touched herself as the memories of Justin's body on top of hers made her tingly and wet. She continued to touch herself for a few minutes but instead of orgasm she burst into tears again and pulled her hand from her pants. She slammed her moist hand down on the bed as an attempt to abruptly stop the memories. It worked momentarily as she stood up from the bed, grabbed her wine glass, gathered her dirty clothes in her arm, and left the room. Once downstairs she put her clothes in the hamper and returned to the caller ID box to see who had called. It was a mixture of calls from Keres, a couple of unknowns, and a few from the Willette Regional Hospital all received that day. Nicolette panicked. Her mind swirled with questions. Did something happen to Lulu? Where was Jamie? How would she get a hold of him to tell him? Maybe he already knew? Maybe he was there with Keres at the hospital and with Lulu already.

Suddenly she thought to call Jamie's work and see if he was there. While she was flipping through the address book on the table for the number, the phone rang again. It was Keres. Nicolette didn't want to have to talk to her but if something happened to Lulu she needed to know. Nicolette picked up the receiver.

"Hello," she said.

"Where the hell is Jamie? I have been trying to get a hold of him all day!" she said.

"Same old Keres," Nicolette mumbled. "Calm down is everything ok? Is Lulu okay?" She asked.

"Lulu is fine you bitch! None of your business! Just tell Jamie to call me!" she said.

Nicolette didn't have a chance to give a response because Keres slammed the phone down and the line disconnected before she could formulate one. Her thoughts moved quickly back to Jamie. If Lulu was okay and he wasn't with Keres, where was he? Why was the hospital calling? Maybe it was Jamie. Nicolette skipped calling his work and pulled up the number for the hospital on the ID box, picked up the phone and dialed the number. It seemed to ring forever until finally a woman from the help desk answered and asked how she could direct the call.

Nicolette explained why she was calling, the lady looked up Jamie's name on the hospital register and connected Nicolette to the correct nurse's station in the hospital. A polite woman answered and asked how she could help. Nicolette once again explained why she was calling. The woman didn't give

Nicolette any information other than yes Jamie was there and suggested Nicolette should probably come down there as soon as she could. Nicolette jotted down the directions she was given, hung up the phone, grabbed her purse, and ran out the front door.

When she arrived at the hospital Nicolette learned Jamie had been in a near-fatal car accident that day in the rain as she said goodbye to Justin. Jamie's vehicle had been sideswiped by a truck driving too fast on the slick roads. She watched Jamie as he laid in his bed hooked up to tubes and machines. It brought back the horror of the day Mitchell died. Nicolette didn't get a chance to be there for Mitchell because he didn't survive but Jamie did. Nicolette didn't have too much experience in receiving loyalty from other people but somehow, she gave it freely and reflexively to others, especially to people who might not deserve it. Her loyalty kicked into high gear for Jamie that day and she stayed by his side at the hospital until he was released.

Chapter Seventeen

Jamie came home from the hospital after a couple of weeks. He had a long road of recovery ahead of him and he wouldn't be able to work for several months while he healed. The large settlement he was scheduled to receive would cover medical expenses and his car with quite a bit leftover. Nicolette took a leave of absence from the Rusty Spur to care for him. It was hard for her to be there anyway. The table where she met Justin became a headstone for the day, they said goodbye. Her isolation from the outside world set in fast. Most of the time it was just her and Jamie. The physical exhaustion and lack of sleep from tending to him around the clock started taking its toll.

The only thing that kept Nicolette going while caring

for Jamie were the short calls, text messages, photos,

and videos from Justin during fleeting moments of

rest during his travels. It was the only time she smiled

and laughed. Those moments were dear to her, but it

wasn't enough. Nicolette longed to lay in his arms

and have a real conversation. She wanted to be

desired and missed his skin on hers. The fantasies of

him naked touching her and inside her that once set

her on fire became a source of pain. He was on her

mind every second of every day and it tormented her.

She wanted to be with him so badly and her despair

grew deeper and deeper.

The more time went on the more her memories of

Justin felt like a distant dream. Without interaction

with Maria, Tom and her customers at the bar each

day she simply went through the motions of being

alive but her heart wasn't in it. She felt like a machine. The nihilism which once poisoned her past was once again in the present.

Jamie was on a lot of pain pills since he was busted up pretty bad. Nicolette made his meals, cleaned the house, and did his laundry. Jamie had a hospital bed up in the loft. He was bound to his bed with the exception of physical therapy days when the techs came to the house twice a week. They helped him move around to keep his mobility and range of motion progressing.

Nicolette was also in charge of Jamie's bathing, grooming, medications, and scheduled any necessary outside care. She became the main person to have to deal with Keres directly and juggle Lulu into the mix when Keres needed her to. Nicolette was so overwhelmed she had bouts of vomiting in the mornings. Even if she was exhausted or sick, she had to keep everything going since there was nobody else to do it. Maria had met a man who swept her off her feet and out the state so Nicolette felt as if she was all Jamie had.

One night after Jamie was asleep and Keres had picked up Lulu, Nicolette collapsed on the couch with a glass of wine. Her emotions were all over the place and she couldn't control them. Her drinking had gotten much worse the longer in between her contact with Justin became. It was clear he was married to his work and he would have to fit Nicolette in when time permitted. She tried to understand but she resented him for it. She wanted to fly off and be with him to travel the world while he worked so they could be together but her current responsibilities would not allow that. Nicolette wasn't even certain if Justin would want that. She felt stuck. The one glass of wine turned into two bottles.

Nicolette climbed the stairs to check on Jamie to see if he needed anything. He was fast asleep and she was relieved. Nicolette went back to the couch with her wine and wished Justin was there with her but he wasn't. She sat staring at her phone wishing it would ring but it didn't. She remembered the prescription for Jamie's pain pills she had left in the glove compartment of her car. If he woke up, he would probably need them so she put her phone in her back pocket, carried her wine glass with her, got her keys, and went out into the parking lot to retrieve the pills. Barefoot she maneuvered around stones and twigs on the pavement.

When she tugged on her passenger side door to open it she dropped her wine glass on the ground next to the car and stepped on some of the glass. It cut the bottom of her foot pretty badly. Nicolette collapsed into the front passenger seat of her car and inspected her wound. There was blood everywhere and she didn't have anything to wipe it up with so she put her foot down on the car mat and started to cry. She screamed to the ceiling of her car in despair no longer believing that God was up above it.

"Why is this how things always go? Am I a terrible person? Is this the abuse I deserve? Is it always going to be this way?" she asked.

Nicolette heard her own questions out loud and answered them to herself silently. Yes. It is always going to be that way and yes, it is what she deserved. It was what she had always deserved. Nicolette had remembered the reason she went outside in the first place. To get the bottle of pills. Instead of bringing them inside for Jamie to take she decided she could just take them herself. All of them. Nicolette fumbled to open the compartment and the struggle made her feel more distraught. When it fell open, she clutched the bottle in her hand and sat fighting with the childproof cap to get them open. As she did, she glanced into the glove box and saw the receipt for her car window with Paul's name and his phone number on it. Nicolette stopped what she was doing. She set the pill bottle down on the dashboard, took out her phone from her pocket and dialed Paul's number. It rang four short times and a male voice answered.

"Paul?" she said.

"This is Paul. Nicolette? Is that you?" he asked.

"Yes, this is Nicolette. Paul?" she said.

"Yes Nicolette?" he asked.

"Paul. I need help," she said.

Paul convinced Nicolette to go back into the house to clean and wrap her foot. She put him on speaker mode and set the phone nearby in the downstairs bathroom while she washed her foot in the sink. He told her fishing stories while she wrapped her cut with gauze and a bandage. When he spoke, her head filled with images of a rippling lake, floating in a canoe with a fishing line in the water, and watching fish jump calmed her down. Paul promised if she switched from wine to coffee, he would stay up all night to talk or just listen as long as she needed.

Nicolette told Paul all about Justin and their time together and how much she missed him. She told him about Jamie and his accident, Keres, and Lulu. She cried when she told him how much she missed Maria and how lonely it was without her there to talk to.

Paul listened until she wore herself out and started to yawn. He stayed on the phone while she changed into her nightgown and crawled into bed. Even after her breathing changed and he could tell she had fallen asleep; Paul was still there.

After a couple of months passed Nicolette's frequent vomiting subsided. Jamie was making great progress although he still spent a lot of time in bed. It seemed the more progress he made the angrier he had gotten. There were days Nicolette thought if he was well enough, he would rather get up out of bed and beat her instead of yell at her. They both might have done the same damage only one you can see one and the other one you can't.

Keres had become extremely intrusive and spent a lot of time upstairs with Jamie while Lulu played in her room. She still treated Nicolette awful but Jamie didn't care. Soon she didn't either. It felt like the three of them were the family and Nicolette was just the maid, nurse, and babysitter. At one-point Nicolette finally wondered why she even stayed at all.

One night while they were all upstairs, Nicolette was downstairs sitting on the couch with a glass of wine. With a moment to herself to think she realized her vomiting stopped but she couldn't recall the last time, she had a period. Maybe it was from all of the stress but maybe it was something else and she needed to find out.

Quietly she sneaked from the house, went to the drug store for a pregnancy test, brought it back home, and secretly took it in the bathroom downstairs. It was positive. Nicolette's head spun whilst she put all of the pieces together. The time frames. Her time with Justin. The vomiting. Uncontrollable emotions. She was trying to remember the last time she and Jamie had sex and then she remembered what he had told her the first night they met. The reason he never wore condoms or used any other protection. Jamie had a vasectomy after Lulu was born. His tumultuous relationship with Keres was enough to make him never want to bring another child into the world.

Now that she thought about it, she hadn't used protection with Justin either. It never occurred to her. Nicolette was so used the prior years with Jamie and not having to think about it. Since she hadn't been with anyone since Justin left, she immediately knew it was his. Nicolette panicked. How would she tell Jamie? Did she want to tell Jamie? Would she tell Justin? Would he want to know?

As she cowered in the bathroom Nicolette heard Keres's abrupt loud voice boom through the bathroom door from the living room and then disappear back up the stairs. Nicolette didn't hate anyone but she considered making an exception for Keres. A sudden urge for decision between fight or flight wafted heavily over her and Nicolette knew she had no strength left to fight. She carefully buried the pregnancy test in the trash can like a child hiding a mess they had made.

Once certain she was alone downstairs Nicolette opened the bathroom door, tiptoed carefully to her bedroom, threw some things in a bag, and left the house just the same way she came into it. She was careful to grab Justin's bottle of tequila from the desk drawer before she went. She was saving it for when he came back for her.

Nicolette ran to the lot, got into her car, stopped for gas, and got onto the highway determined this time to leave Willette behind instead of run to it. As she drove, she reminisced about the last leg of her journey the day she arrived there. She remembered thinking more cars were leaving Willette then were driving beside her towards it. After her time there it occurred to her maybe they too were running from something they desperately needed to leave behind somewhere within the city limits of Willette.

With each mile, Nicolette began to feel stronger about her decision to go. She had been so scared for so long to start over without Jamie. There were many times she wanted to leave but fear of the unknown kept her stagnant. Jamie was so much like her father but somehow it was the familiarity she clung too. Nicolette wasn't sure what would happen when Jamie found out she was gone but for once she cared more about her own survival than his and she was determined to never see Jamie again.

The short time Nicolette spent with Justin had given her a new standard to strive for and the idea she was valuable. She could no longer settle for just getting by. Although he wasn't there with her now, the life she carried inside her was part of him and it gave her hope for the future. As she drove, she struggled with how to tell him her secret and wondered how he would react. When her cell phone illuminated on the seat next to her and began to ring it startled her. It was Justin. Nicolette's heart began to race. She had daydreamed of scenarios and rehearsed conversations in her mind a million times yet still terrified it was about to happen. Nicolette picked up the phone and was shaking as she pushed the button to answer. Her voice quivered when she spoke.

"Justin," she said.

"Hey, you. How are you?" he said.

"A lot has happened Justin and I really need to talk to you. I miss you," she said.

"I only have a few minutes and the cell phone service here is terrible. If I lose you I will call you next chance I get," he said.

"Where are you?" she asked.

The phone crackled and she couldn't understand Justin's response.

"Justin I am pregnant," she said.

Again, the phone crackled as he spoke just before the call dropped. Nicolette wasn't sure if Justin heard what she had said. She tried to call back the number but it went straight to voicemail so she hung up.

Nicolette doubted a voicemail was such a great way to tell him what she had to say. It would obviously have to wait.

Nicolette turned up the radio, Glen Campbell was belting out Rhinestone Cowboy like a boss and she lost herself in a song for the first time in a long time. When Nicolette was young her grandparents had taken her to lunch at a local pub where Nicolette learned to shoot pool. They had a small room filled with arcade games she played until she ran out of quarters. Her grandfather gave her a handful more so she could choose some songs to listen to on the jukebox while they ate their lunch. One of the songs she chose was Rhinestone Cowboy and she was hooked from then on. As Nicolette sang along at the top of her lungs the stress poured off of her. She was startled when the interior of the car illuminated with the cell phone light. Once again it was Justin. Nicolette scrambled to turn down the radio and started to pull to the side of the highway as she answered.

"Hello," she said.

"Nicolette, sorry the call dropped it might happen again so let me hurry. I have some good news," he said.

Nicolette's mind raced. She wondered what the news could be and also if Justin had heard what she told him before they were disconnected the last time but she didn't ask.

"Ok," she said.

"I got signed on this new gig and it will be a lot of touring but it's a really great opportunity. I don't really have any time to do it but not everyone gets these opportunities so I feel like I should take them when they come along. Isn't it great?" he said.

Nicolette's heart slowly sank into her stomach when she sensed he hadn't heard her news. Part of her started to shake at the thought of having to say it out loud again. The other part of her was really happy for him. If anyone deserved these opportunities it was him. He worked hard to get where he was and he was a good person too. She certainly didn't want to be the reason he changed his whole life he seemed to enjoy.

"That is great Justin! I am so happy for you," she said.

"It will be quite a while before I can make it back to Willette but we can try and get together any time I come near there. You know just living life," he said.

Nicolette held the phone away from her face towards the passenger side door and started to cry, took a couple of deep breaths and brought it back to her ear.

"Nicolette?" he asked.

"Yes. Yeah, I am here. No that is wonderful news. Sure, we can work all this stuff out somehow. No problem. Just keep in touch when you can," she said.

"Ok well I have to go I am supposed to go on in five minutes. I will call when I can. Goodnight Nicolette," he said.

"Goodbye Justin," she said.

The rest of her drive felt even longer after talking to Justin but she pushed through stopping a few times for gas, food, and to use the restroom along the way. Finally, she arrived at a familiar exit she hadn't seen in so long. She was looking for someone. Although she didn't know the address, she thought she knew where to look. Nicolette pulled into the motel parking lot across the road from Denny's restaurant. Her eyes scanned for a big truck with the word Sheriff on the door and she found it sitting in the back of the lot where they had first met. A man with a light-colored cowboy hat leaned against it with his head down writing something in a small notepad.

Nicolette parked her car in a space near to him, got out, and started walking towards him across the lot. She was tired and worn and broken and she didn't know where else to go. Her pace increased the closer she got to him. Paul looked up from his notepad and first a look of shock came over his face which turned quickly to a smile. He set the notepad down on the hood of his truck, turned to Nicolette and outstretched his arms. Nicolette collapsed against his chest as his arms enveloped her. Paul stroked her head gently

with his palm and they held each other tight.